The Vessel

Books by
Adam L. G. Nevill

Novels

Banquet for the Damned

Apartment 16

The Ritual

Last Days

House of Small Shadows

No One Gets Out Alive

Lost Girl

Under a Watchful Eye

The Reddening

Cunning Folk

The Vessel

Short Story Collections

Some Will Not Sleep

Hasty for the Dark

Wyrd and Other Derelictions

The Vessel

Adam L. G. Nevill

Ritual Limited
Devon, England
MMXXII

The Vessel

by Adam L. G. Nevill

Published by
Ritual Limited
Devon, England
MMXXII
www.adamlgnevill.com

Cover design by The Dead Good Design Company Limited
Cover artwork by Samuel Araya
Text design by The Dead Good Design Company Limited
Ritual Limited logo by Moonring Art Design
Printed and bound by Amazon KDP
ISBN 978-1-7397886-1-2

For Julie Crisp, who rolled the dice.

'I believe that something unseen is also here'

Walt Whitman, 'Song of the Open Road'

I

A stillness profound enough to be uncanny hushes a woodland glade. Trees encircle the placid water of a circular pond therein, the surface a black mirror reflecting a sombre sky.

Glimpsed between the columns of trunks and downy birch branches that ring the water, white blossom and vivid flowers erupt along the borders of a distant lawn. Beyond this mown pelt of grass, a weathered vicarage stands sentinel. An outcrop of dour stone with windows as impenetrable as the pond's untroubled surface.

The atmosphere of mournful tranquillity is only disturbed when a cat appears upon the lawn to stalk a thrush. As it closes upon its prey, the cries of the other birds at a safer height grow shrill.

Behind a French window in the vicarage, the pale smudge of a face peers out. The surrounding void of the unlit room offers vague definition to a withered head. A woman, her white hair thinning, whose face appears disembodied, suspended in darkness. Morose yet expectant, she watches the confrontation on the lawn.

Reflected upon the pupils of her rheumy eyes, the thrush explodes from the lawn. A sudden flight inciting a fresh orchestra of avian shrieks from the wings of this outdoor theatre. The pupils of the watcher at the window quickly become busier with more black shapes, swooping upon the hunter, until a cat's scream of rage and terror tears the air. The hunted bird's wings flap-crack in a soaring escape.

Vicarage, garden, wood and pond grow smaller below the reprieved thrush. It sees the land become a patchwork in which the suggestion of a circular village, with the vicarage forming the hub of an indistinct wheel, assumes shape.

Black clouds cover the world.

Within an hour, the thrush descends from a sooty sky, its keen sight fixing upon a housing estate where busy roads encircle cement blocks, and the air is a brown haze. Closing claws upon the railing of a gantry in a grubby block of flats, the bird sees the face of another careworn woman, who sits in silence behind a kitchen window.

2

*J*ess looks out of the kitchen window without taking any notice of the world. She searches inwardly to gather the resolve and strength required for the day ahead. With fingers reddened by cleaning agents, she habitually worries an old scar that cuts her top lip and extends to her nose.

Outside the flat, the hostile sounds that she has learned to background are unrelenting. A scooter revs. A door slams in a communal corridor. A dog barks incessantly as if driven mad. Above the ceiling of the flat, the thump of dance music pounds a tribal rhythm.

Jess drops her hands to her lap where her fingers, with their bitten-down nails, twist and entwine upon the glossy estate agent's brochure spread upon her lap. The cover features an artist's impression of a pristine cedar-panelled housing block. A dream destination of huge windows and balconies set in a grassy park where the graphics of conjured children frolic. 'New Development. Family Homes.'

In contrast to the comforts the pamphlet promises, this kitchen's interior can only reveal the evidence of a mother's attempts to make a space contemporary and homely with cheap, bright pictures and feature walls. In two corners, an intrusion of black-spore fungus persists in discolouring her efforts to enliven the room. When her gaze returns to the brochure, an expression of longing that seems painful induces her to hold her disfigured lip between her teeth.

She eventually stirs from her absorption and glances at the doorway that opens onto the kitchen. 'Izzy, love! We'll be late. My first day!' And to herself, 'We need this.'

When the small figure of her daughter shuffles into the doorway, Jess tucks the brochure inside her bag.

Izzy enters the room with a slow, determined reluctance. Her auburn hair, brushed into tight bunches, is also tied with pink bows.

Jess finds her daughter's pale and nervy expression too hard to look at. It is too similar for comfort to the very image of herself that she has been gazing at, on the inside of the kitchen window. And though her daughter's dressed neatly, Jess's eyes cannot refrain from dwelling upon the tired aspects of Izzy's school uniform. A faded cardigan repaired with a different blue wool to the garment's original fabric, complemented by school shoes, the toes worn grey, the remaining uppers polished to a dull shine.

Jess reaches onto the counter and rummages inside one of her daughter's three bags. 'These the right books?'

Izzy nods, unhappily.

Jess shakes a drink-bottle to make sure it's full. Then holds up a nylon bag by the string handle. 'Kit I just washed?'

Izzy nods again.

Jess slides off the stool, wets a finger and dabs at a toothpaste stain on her daughter's cardigan. Only then does Izzy break a silence that has survived since she was last in the kitchen to push a spoon at her soggy cereal, half an hour before. 'Penny picking me up from school?'

'Me this week, love.'

On receipt of the information, Izzy's eyes brighten. But not by much. 'No more nights for Mummy?'

Jess tugs up her sleeve to check the time. 'Not if I can help it.' She looks back at her daughter and frowns at what she reads in Izzy's eyes. They glisten with tears. 'Hey. What's all this?'

Prompted by a query into her misery, Izzy looks at the floor and starts to cry.

Jess embraces her daughter. Eyes screwed shut from the intense concern that squeezes everything inside her chest, she kisses her daughter and lets her lips linger upon the child's warm forehead.

'I feel poorly,' Izzy manages through her sobs.

'Them kids up your school again?'

'Can I stay with Mummy today?'

'My love. You know you can't. Any more trouble from them, I'm coming to see the head teacher again. Sick of it.' When Izzy's sobs subside to sniffles, Jess breaks the clinch and dabs at her daughter's eyes. 'My little love. Things gonna get better for us. Soon. I promise. And guess what?'

Izzy is too desolate to raise a smidgen of interest.

'Got a surprise for you Thursday. We're going somewhere special.' Her mother's voice carries a bright, artificial ring.

'Where?'

'Surprise. Like I said.'

'Where though?'

'Wait till Thursday. But maybe you won't be going to that school much longer.'

Izzy stops sniffing. On receipt of such impossible news, that is too cruel to fully entertain, her eyes lock upon her mother's face and search for insincerity, for tricks, or those infuriating postscripts about being patient.

'Till then, stay away from them kids. Walk away. Ignore them. Hide if you have to. Only thing that works with bullies is to keep well out their way. Little bas—' Jess reaches for Izzy again and indulges the small form with a final hug that fuses the child to her chest. 'But we gotta go now if you want to make Early-Bird Club.'

'Love you, Mummy.'

'Love you more than anything in this world, Izz. Even more than ice-cream.'

Wet eyes sparkling, Izzy laughs and snuffles up the last of her tears.

'C'mon. Let's get cracking.'

Scrabbling up keys and swiping a phone from a counter and looping all three of her daughter's bags along one forearm, before snagging their coats from a little rack in the reception, Jess herds her daughter out of the flat.

As the front door opens, the barking of the dog amplifies within the communal corridor. Jess and Izzy hesitate and briefly peer between cement walls painted yellow before falling into a quick step towards the staircase.

3

With the finality of a prison gate, the thick security door of the block's main entrance slams behind Jess and Izzy, shudders in the frame, then locks with a click.

'Daddy!' Izzy bursts into a run, her rucksack slapping and bunches flying.

Startled, Jess jerks around – the very word 'Daddy' triggering a reaction that most would read as panic if they were to look into her eyes. A response she stifles. Face hardening, she's powerless to do anything but watch Tony spread his arms as Izzy ploughs into him and buries her face in her father's stomach. Staggering backwards to exaggerate the impact of the collision, Tony laughs. Blue plastic bags, looped from each of Tony's hands, sway like bells.

'You in the school rugby team? Blimey, you pack a punch. You grow an inch every day I'm away, kitten.' Tony kneels and, closing his eyes, folds around his daughter, kissing the top of her head.

Izzy pulls back and eyes the bags hanging from her father's wrists. Her smile grows coy. 'What's that? Something for me?'

Warily, Jess closes on them. 'Izz. We're late.'

Tony and Izzy ignore her. Tony rummages inside the bag and produces a bag of crisps. Izzy seizes them. He whips out a chocolate bar, followed by a bag of jellies, a deli wrap, an apple. Izzy laughs, her little hands snatching.

'Keep you goin', eh? Make you even more beautiful. Specially that apple. Snow White apple. Red like you love.'

Jess sighs but seems ready to scream. 'It ain't . . . Tone. You can't just . . .'

Tony kisses Izzy on top of the head producing a loud smacking noise. He points to the car behind him. 'Go have a look inside, Izz. In the back. Fixed it. Like new.'

Izzy runs to the car and peers through the rear window. 'My bike! Mummy, my bike!'

Tony turns to Jess. 'Sorry, luv. I know. I know. I shouldn't have come but it breaks my heart if I go a day without her.'

'It's hard. But they said—'

'I know. Gotta be another way, though. It's all I think of.'

'I gotta get on. Work.'

'You carry on. I'll drop Izz at school. No strings. Least I'll get to see her for a bit.'

It's the first time that morning that Jess has seen her daughter's face split by a smile, though her only child's happiness fails to revive similar feelings in her.

'Yes, Mum. Yes, Mum. I want to go in Daddy's car!'

Tony grins, sheepish. 'It'll make my whole day.'

Jess's grim smile battles irritation. She manages to nod at her ecstatic daughter.

Tony pushes his pitch into a wheedling softness that turns his voice breathy. 'You both do. Every time I see you. Even for a minute or two. Ain't forgot Mum neither.' Tony pushes the second bag towards Jess. She looks at it but doesn't accept the offering.

'Little something. Don't mean nothing.'

Jess takes the bag, eyeing it with a distaste often seen on the faces of dog walkers as they straighten their backs in the park with a plastic bag held at arm's length.

'Drop you off?'

She shakes her head.

At the rebuttal, remorse makes Tony appear younger.

Though the sigh and sympathetic nod that follow suggest the sagacity of an older man. He turns about and scoops up his daughter.

'Can I ride it outside school?'

'If we get a move on.'

Jess surreptitiously peers inside the bag drooping from her fingertips and sees a box of Black Magic chocolates. An apple. A handwritten envelope containing a greeting card. As if throttling a chicken, she wrings the neck of the bag shut.

The doors of Tony's car close. Izzy's laughter dims then mutes as the passenger side is sealed, leaving Jess in a suddenly greyer world. Traffic shudders on the main road. A car horn blares. A distant siren suggests that someone else's day has endured a start far worse than her own. Small comfort.

4

At the crowded bus stop, indifferent faces surround Jess. Eyes hard and minds preoccupied with their own struggles on another grey day, chilled by the cold damp air. A bleak piece of waste ground lies behind a chain-link fence, parallel to the queue. A distant industrial estate cramps the horizon. A few feet from the bus shelter, a muscular dog dumps a crap on the scruffy verge. Its squat owner doesn't pick up the steaming mess and plods on, surly and huffing.

A petulant moped screams amidst the grinding traffic. Another two buzz in pursuit. In the brazen din of their engines, Jess can't hear her phone ring but the handset vibrates against her hip. She hurriedly extracts it from her jacket and looks at the screen.

'Oh, piss off.' She answers the call with a fake smile. 'Sheila. How are—'

'I would imagine you're there now.'

Jess winces. 'Nearly. On the bus—'

'Cutting it fine.'

'I—'

'This morning's call is to emphasise how important a client Mrs Gardner is to this agency. So, under no circumstances – and I mean this, Jess – can there be a repeat of what happened last time.'

'Like I already said, Sheila, stuff's in place. With custody. And me and Izzy are looking to move—'

'So I'm reminding you of the assurance you gave me that your personal problems won't affect your work. Again. This includes punctuality.'

At Jess's elbow in the bus stop, a man snaps opens a can of cider and she flinches as if a gun has gone off next to her head. Instinctively, her hand covers the lower half of her face and she fingers the scar bisecting her top lip. As if she's turned the volume of the world down a few notches, Sheila's voice fades. Only to rise again with a tone sharpened by exasperation. 'Are you listening?'

'Yeah. Yes. And I'm grateful for the job . . . opportunity, Sheila. I need this. Izzy needs—'

'You have your notes. Morag will brief you on the rest.'

As Jess scratches amongst thoughts scattered by the eruption of the cider can, to cobble together the assurance her employer seeks, Sheila ends the call.

The bus arrives and shudders to a halt. The queue collapses into a scrum about the doors.

Jess doesn't move and stands apart from the disorder.

5

 athed in sunlight golden enough to conjure a fancy
that she might have stepped into another world, one
she'd forgotten could exist, Jess walks tree-softened
Sheaf Lane.

She might also have been painted into a fine artist's vista.
Each detached period building in the village of Eadric rears
proudly behind a lawn as flat as a bowling green, or stands
knee-deep in the kind of floral displays that are awarded
trophies at flower shows. Tree blossom further enchants an
atmosphere likely to arrest even the most preoccupied mind
walking through it. And suffering no competition from traffic
or human congress, only the fluting and whistling of birdsong
pierces the warm air.

A little dazed, Jess peers at the wisteria-wreathed porches
to identify numbers on houses that seem intent on being
identified by individual names. Nerthus House is the one she
seeks.

A sign on the garden wall of the sixth house on the
left, The Old Vicarage, indicates that it is Nerthus House.
A building so grand, yet imperiously sombre, that Jess is
impelled to check the first page of the folder she carries to
make sure it's the right address. But this is it. Where she's
supposed to be. Handsome but funereal Nerthus House.

Self-conscious, she dithers as two elderly women pass on
the other side of Sheaf Lane, each accompanied by a small
dog. Her surprise turning to deference, Jess tidies her hair and

appraises her simple, functional outfit. The women pause to study the outsider, increasing her discomfort. Unsure whether to laugh nervously or apologise for daring to find herself somewhere so pretty and old and affluent, Jess looks at the dog walkers.

Who walk on without a word.

She turns back to the vicarage and approaches the front door, moving as she might between the aisles of an old library favoured by fierce scholars.

Behind her back, the two elderly pedestrians pause and watch her until the front door of Nerthus House opens.

6

A burly form fills the doorway. The severe expression on the woman's broad, doughy face appears permanent and projects enough disapproval across the threshold to fill the porch.

Jess smiles at the looming presence. 'Hi. Morag?'

The night carer that Jess is to relieve is already wearing her coat. 'Didn't Sheila tell you to be here at nine?'

'Sorry. Buses—'

'Cus it's gone half-past and we ain't done the handover yet.' Footnoting the introduction with a scowl, Morag turns her back on Jess and shuffles inside.

Nervous as much as chastened, Jess steps inside Nerthus House and passes from sunlight to be wholly swallowed within a dim, cluttered hallway, the parquet tiles obstructed by bulging plastic bags.

Before her eyes adjust to the thin sepia haze, she trips at the foot of a once elegant staircase, its path upwards vanishing into the gloom of the first storey, the best part of each step buried under the cascade of cardboard boxes and bags that appear to have tumbled from the darkness above.

Jess rights herself and glances through the doorway of a dining room the size of her flat and sees another dim space crowded to capacity with aged furniture, boxes, cases, heaped clothing, more plastic bags made taut by their contents, bales of yellowing newspaper and magazines sloping into disarray.

A mound of stacked, dust-furred belongings forms the centrepiece of the room, built around a dining table rendered near invisible by the obstructions. The structure resembles the kind of crude playhouse that a child would make indoors were it allowed to use every stick of furniture and possession at hand in its construction. A dark mouth at the front of the pile suggests the door of a burrow, or barrow.

Nerthus House is the home of a shut-in: a dark warren that hasn't been cleared, let alone tidied. In years.

Jess fails to conceal her horror at what she's seeing in such poor, unhealthy light. 'I don't understand.'

'Eh?'

'It's . . . I mean . . . Not very dementia-friendly?'

'How Mrs Gardner wanted it. You can't touch nothing neither. Ain't you read the notes?'

'Yeah. Course. But this . . .'

'All you gotta worry about is the living room, kitchen, her bedroom, bathroom. Rest is off-limits.'

'Can't be right. Who's the appointee? Who's got power of attorney?'

'Ask Sheila. Got nothing to do with me.' Impatient with the interrogation, Morag stamps into the chaotic kitchen at the front of the house, expecting Jess to follow.

As if infected by the disorder of the vicarage, the night-worker hasn't cleaned up after herself in a while either. Dirty crockery litters counter-tops and fills the sink. An accumulation of grime on each side of the kitchen windows strains the sunlight a dusty brown and adds decades to the already dated cabinets and appliances.

As Morag pockets her phone and hurriedly throws items into her bag, Jess eyes an untidy pile of medication boxes, stacked on the counter just inside the doorway. 'Memantine Hydrochloride?'

Morag doesn't look up. 'What she's been prescribed. Diary's there.'

'Antipsychs aren't in the notes.'

'Hallucinations have come back. She's feisty when she's disturbed. Make sure she gets it.'

'Better light might help her for a start. I mean . . .' With a nod, Jess indicates the visible gloom.

'You a doctor? Didn't fink so. You ain't even a nurse.'

'State of this place though.'

'Do as we're told. She's fourth age anyway. You won't be here long.'

'Charming. Family?'

'She ain't had a single visitor since I been here. Three years and counting. She's through here. I gotta get on.'

7

*B*eyond the indiscernible features of the living room, the open French windows at the far end of the large space create a rectangle of intense golden light that appears contained there. Light that frames a glimpse of the rear garden's wild foliage while failing to illumine much of the room. The dazzle forces Jess to squint and raise a hand to shield her eyes.

Partially eclipsing the glow in the lower half of the French windows sits the black silhouette of a shrunken figure within a wheelchair: Mrs Florence Gardner.

Despite the voices and commotion of the carers who enter the room, the client continues to stare outside, her thinning, unkempt hair a fuzzy halo. As dishevelled as her home, the client is dressed in a shabby velvet leisure suit and old slippers.

Crossing the room and seeing more of the high-ceilinged space, Jess's bewilderment becomes wonder. Evidence abounds of the cultivated tastes and affluence of a long and privileged life reduced to a dust-filmed museum exhibit. A space overfilled with hardwood furniture and bookcases. The available walls are festooned with oils, line drawings and watercolours. A vast fireplace suggests the door to an unlit tunnel. Before the grate, the dull iron of a barbed fire-poker lies upon a basket of cobwebbed firewood. Next to the French windows, antique dinnerware and silverware glimmer inside the murk of a broad, glass-fronted cabinet.

The only vital feature here is the beautiful garden that lies beyond the room. Jess wanders towards the vista. In such light as falls here she might be admiring a watercolour by Monet.

Her scrutiny is drawn across the lawn to the climax of the visible garden, where her vision rests upon a wooded glade, part-glimpsed between columns of trees.

The way the light drops into the grove, before spilling outwards as if dispersed by a powerful mirror, issues a curious sense of the sacred and hallowed that she finds immediately affecting. Her admiration for that distant beauty, and what feels like an affinity with it, appears with a warm familiarity, without her knowing exactly why. It's as if something is being withheld, like a compelling memory just out of the reach of her recall.

Reluctantly turning her gaze from the vision of the glade beyond the garden, she steps to the chair and searches Mrs Gardner's murky eyes. They continue to comb the distant tree-line. Still mystified by the strength of her own reaction to the glade, she identifies the same childlike adoration in Mrs Gardner's expression; a fascination that she feels she shares without any precise idea of how and why that arrangement of trees is so irresistible. Jess looks out again, both carer and client now peering at the trees together, Flo yearning, Jess mystified yet seduced by such beauty.

Only Morag's introduction, which aspires to a bellow, destroys Jess's preoccupation. 'Blossom! New girl's here! Jess! She's gonna look after you for a bit. I gotta get on.'

It is then, as Jess turns from the light, that she catches sight of the slack, unbuckled restraints on the footplate and arms of the patient's wheelchair. Her horror prompts her to search Morag's face and silently implore the older carer for an explanation.

Morag scowls. 'Legs is all stiff and she can't walk no more. But she can be quick with her hands. Gotta watch 'em. Had a stroke three years ago. Ain't much facial expression so you get no warning, like.'

'She's eighty-nine.'

Jess kneels before Flo's wheelchair and makes sure she has eye contact. She smiles. Placing a hand gently on Flo's withered claw, the yellowing nails too long untrimmed, she speaks softly to her new client. 'Hello, my love. I've never seen such a pretty garden. I know just what my little girl would say if she saw it. She'd say, Mummy, I bet fairies live here.'

Agitated before Jess finishes speaking, Flo pulls her hand away and returns her gaze to the glade. Her stare intensifies, perhaps with an expectation, as if she waits for someone to appear.

Disappointed with the rebuff, Jess turns her head as if led by Flo's stare to the garden.

SMACK.

Flo's hand connects with the side of Jess's head. Lumpy fingers entangle in her hair. A veiny old fist closes, yanking hard, pulling Jess face-down.

Using both hands to peel her hair from Flo's grasp, Jess shrieks and wriggles backwards until her knee strikes a jug beside Flo's chair. The jug discharges blackcurrant squash like a flood of old blood.

Morag thumps in and tears roughly at Jess's hair to snap it from Flo's gnarled fingers. With limited success. The scuffle progresses into a clumsy, humiliating catfight between the three women: two carers fighting an elderly, disabled dementia patient.

When Jess is eventually freed, a flushed Morag dusts Jess's uprooted hair from the palms of her hands while glaring at her new colleague, as if it is she who is at fault. 'What I just tell ya! Jesus.'

Dazed, Jess bends to right the jug.

The motion it instigates is nothing but a blur at the edge of her vision as Flo thrusts forward from the waist and swipes a bony fist at Jess's face.

CRUNCH.

The punch knocks Jess's head from east to west. White noise and bright flashes shatter her awareness of the room and her position within it. She staggers from the chair, then crumples. Dazed from the blow, she recovers enough to find herself sat on her backside on the wet carpet, her eyes wide with shock and hair in disarray. She can only gape in horror and disbelief at Morag and then Flo, the two figures backgrounded by what resembles a seldom visited museum.

When she shakes off her concussed stupor, she lurches to her feet and races from the room, her tatty hair extending wildly.

8

*J*ess holds up her makeup mirror with palsied fingers but can do little more than scrape at strands of hair in an attempt to flatten them. Inside the magnifying mirror, the scar that disfigures her mouth looms bigger and uglier.

Can I stay with Mummy today?

One hand pressed against the counter for support, the second across her disfigured mouth, Jess muffles her distress so that Morag won't hear.

And hither comes that consuming image of Izzy as an infant, standing inside a baby-walker in the doorway of the small kitchen in their flat. A vivid memory from early motherhood, and never welcome when recalled. Izzy is crying hard. Real tears upon a face red and creased with the confused terror that a child feels harder than anyone. And beyond the recollection of her infant's urgent cries, she hears the football match that was playing on the television in the next room.

A blood-sodden tea towel discarded on a kitchen counter.

A knocked-out human tooth at the bottom of a metal sink.

Jess sniffs, dabs her eyes with the back of her hands, then a sleeve. Takes a deep breath that shudders. Closes her eyes and counts to ten before turning for the door.

Embarrassed, her composure frail and posture stiff, she returns to the living room.

Flo watches the garden as if nothing unusual has occurred.

Morag dabs a cloth in a frenzy at the dark stain on the carpet before the wheelchair. She looks up briefly and eyes Jess with pity and disdain, her confidence in the new girl shot. 'Everything you need's in the diary.' Morag struggles to her feet, then bustles from the room without another word.

Still stunned, Jess drifts after her on unsteady legs.

Morag snatches up her bag from a kitchen counter, thuds into the hall, swings wide the front door and steps out.

Dabbing her eyes and still attempting to neaten her hair and reclaim some dignity, Jess shuffles after her new colleague, up to the threshold. But pauses when the flood of morning light pours through the front door and blinds her. 'Hang on. Sheila tell you I need to go at two, Thursday?'

'Yeah. Skiving already. She told you, you's on nights next two shifts?'

'No chance. Picking me daughter up.'

'I'm not here. You'll have to rearrange it.'

'Can't – not childcare at short notice.'

'You'll have to bring it up with Sheila. And don't touch the chicken in the fridge. That's my tea.'

'Hang on!'

'You already showed up late! I ain't got time to argue on the doorstep.' Morag pulls the door closed and returns Jess to the gloom. Dusty light struggles through the stained glass above the door: a spoked wheel of gold, or depiction of the sun. Weak threads of red and green extend into the cluttered throat of the vicarage. Jess turns and stares into the dark.

9

*O*n the playground, a barrage of sound assails Izzy. She stands alone, and from near and far the howls and chitters and shrieks, which could have been issued by confined apes and birds, deflect from the cement and glass of the school buildings.

She is mute, uncomfortable and unsmiling, but her eyes are alight with fascination. Standing at the edge of a wide tarmac play area – the gritty surface scored by faint lines once a vivid white, pink, red and green – she tries to interpret the exciting maelstrom she's excluded from.

So engrossed is she by the congress of the morning break, she's unaware of what is transpiring behind her back as three grinning girls creep close and assemble in a line, taking care to stay outside of their prey's peripheral vision.

A child's arm, clad in a blue cardigan sleeve, dips inside the aperture where the zipper parts at the top of Izzy's rucksack. The arm returns to the air, the small hand grasping the bag of jelly sweets that Tony gave her that morning.

Another small hand, the fingers stained by felt-tip pens, takes a turn and stealthily prods inside the dark hollow of Izzy's unzipped bag, returning with the chocolate bar.

Izzy doesn't move. She's entranced by playtime, this intense milling, the arcane rituals of games, groups, hierarchies and interaction. But when a third pair of hands delicately, though audaciously, attempts to unclip the fluffy Beanie Boo unicorn

31

affixed to a strap on Izzy's bag, the thief's excitement results in a tug at the toy and the rucksack moves.

Behind Izzy a girl laughs. Another sucks in her breath. Izzy swivels around and confronts the sneak-thieves.

Confusion transforming to fear, she does nothing but stare at the three girls. Caught red-handed, the girl seemingly fused to her rucksack is all too familiar to Izzy. She's grinning and clutching the attached unicorn with an intention that fills her victim with dread. The girl's grubby hands unclip the toy.

Izzy's eyes flare with alarm and she pulls at the bag to deter the thief. 'Leave it!'

The pickpocket grins in triumph. Izzy snatches at the unicorn but her tormentor is too quick and steps away, holding her loot aloft. She and her two friends turn, race away. Noisy as a flock of gulls with chip wrappers, they shriek elatedly. The rhythmic slapping of their feet fades.

'It's mine!' Izzy pursues them, her open bag flapping about her back like a sloppy mouth. When she gains on the girl with the toy, she seizes the child's loose cardigan and pulls her up.

Instantly furious, the girl turns and grabs Izzy's arm and swings her around in a semi-circle. Losing her balance, then her footing, Izzy slaps down upon her side. Like sandpaper, the tarmac scrapes her chin, and her face is at once rendered wet and hot and stinging.

When her breath returns she sits up but finds herself still arrested by shock. She gazes at a cut hand and a grazed knee flooding crimson. From her glowing chin falls a drip-drop-drip-drop onto her pleated skirt. Bulbs of shiny blood that soak black into her cotton lap. The sight of the blood finally breaks her trance and ushers her tears.

Inside her blurred vision, the three bullies dodge away into the din and chaos of play. And the sound of Izzy's heart-deep despair is absorbed by the contained, frustrated wildness of this compound.

10

inally composed and determined to restart her assignment, her face washed and hair neatened, Jess carries a tray laden with a well-presented lunch to her client. Chicken sandwiches and salad.

'Found a nice bit of chicken in the fridge, Flo. Diary says you have early lunch but not what you like. Can't go wrong with chicken though. Bit of salad.'

Jess places the tray on a stand and rolls it over to Flo's wheelchair, her movements slowing with wariness. She then strides to the windows and tugs the stiff, heavy curtains open. Shoves a window wide. Nets billow. The room lightens.

Jess swings back across the room and switches off the television that no one is watching. 'Don't know what they're thinking, leaving you in the dark all day. What this house needs is sunlight. Lot of it.'

She pauses near the cabinet, the murky contents briefly snagging her attention. Under closer scrutiny, what resembled a collection of rubble becomes a scattering of broken artefacts. Archaeological evidence, fragments of ancient peoples that line several shelves: an amateur's collection of potsherds, an array of corroded coins, beads made from brass, a weathered buckle or brooch featuring a spoked wheel or depiction of the sun, similar to the fanlight above the front door.

Her scrutiny drifts along the unlabelled artefacts until pausing upon a twisted, leathery object. A gnarled thing that resembles an ancient glove. A blackened hand-shape with several fingers missing.

Wincing in distaste, and a little mystified as to why anyone would want such a thing on display in a living room, she returns to the wheelchair in which Flo stares aimlessly at the garden, her eyes blank. Kneeling at a safe distance, Jess takes cutlery from a napkin.

SMASH.

'Christ!' The plate is upended and the food that Jess has carefully prepared bounces and scatters about her legs.

Flo withdraws her hand and drops it on her lap. 'Useless bitch!'

In shock at such ferocity from the elderly woman, Jess blinks her eyes rapidly. Her ears ring from the depth and force of her client's voice.

Gingerly, she bends forward to pick up the articles of bread and salad strewn before the footplate of the chair.

The very moment she takes her eyes off her client a spitting sound issues wetly from above her head. And across her face a stream of lumpy saliva patters.

Near paralysed with shock, and now disgust, Jess does little but straighten her back and blink at the spittle lacing her forehead, one eyelid and cheek. She wipes the back of a hand across her eyes. Flo returns her agitated gaze to the garden and immediately calms.

Fists clenched and arms corded, Jess exerts all of her willpower to restrain herself from lashing out at the abusive spitter in the wheelchair. Face aquiver and bloodless, she rises to her feet and eyes the unused straps on the armrests and footplate of the wheelchair, before withdrawing from the room in silence, patting her cheek with a sleeve.

For the second time in one morning after crossing the threshold of Nerthus House, she's back inside the kitchen, shaking with emotion. One side of her face is still bright red and the corresponding eye is watering.

She dabs the spittle from her face and fringe with a dish cloth. Once she's removed as much as she can find, she yanks open the kitchen cupboards and discovers the shelves to be stocked with cheap, plain biscuits. 'Might have known. Bloody biscuits.'

Tearing at cellophane, she commits her anger to opening the packet. When the top tier of biscuits drops and smashes on the floor, she stares at the shards as if even the food in this place is designed to wilfully defy her.

She crosses the hall, kicks aside a bulging plastic bag and marches into the living room. Drawing a deep breath, she approaches Flo's chair and calmly rights the portable tray so she can place the open packet of biscuits before Flo. As if confronting a dangerous animal, she maintains an arm's length of distance during the procedure.

The old woman's claw swiftly extends to snatch and seize a biscuit. Flo then nips at her prize with rapid bites. An unappealing, feral process that encourages Jess to back further away.

The biscuit consumed, Flo's face is transformed by a faint smile. 'I hope we can be friends. Cup of tea, mother.'

Baffled, Jess retreats to the kitchen.

Leaning over the sink, with her hands placed wide apart and shoulders slumped, she closes her eyes. As she tries to come down from the trauma and confusion of an awful morning, the melodious voice of a happy child out front distracts her.

Across the lane, a mother and a blonde girl around Izzy's age, wearing the chic uniform of a private school, gather beside a performance car. A handsome, well-dressed duo bidding goodbye to a storybook grandmother who wears a wide-brimmed straw hat. Around the three generations of this well-heeled family, a garden blooms, framing perfection.

Jess turns from the window to consult the diary as the car pulls away. Once it has purred beyond Nerthus House, the elderly neighbour remains in her garden but no longer watches the departing car. Instead, she stares at the vicarage, the look in her eyes fearfully stern. Her teeth are visible, as if the figure with the perfectly still body is grimacing.

Though Jess is aware of the woman at the corner of her eye, her phone trills before she can meet the neighbour's persistent gaze. She flinches as if struck or spat at again. 'Christ.'

As the device rarely brings good news, Jess peers at her phone screen with a pained resignation until, sure enough, she reads IZZY SCHOOL lit up on the screen.

'Sorry to bother you at work, Mrs McMachen.'

'What's wrong?'

'I don't want you to worry. It's nothing serious. But Isabelle's with the nurse. She's had an accident.'

'What?'

From the phone jammed against her ear, the matter-of-fact tone of the voice bewilders Jess even more than the information the school receptionist is imparting. The woman might be mentioning a missing PE kit. 'There was an incident with another child. The Head thinks you should come in. She'd like a chat. Can you come in this afternoon?'

Jess drifts into the hallway and gapes at the living room and at her incapacitated client whom she can't leave until Morag comes in for the night shift. 'I can't get away till six earliest. I'm a carer. For a dementia patient.'

After that call ends, others are initiated by an increasingly frantic Jess, who paces the narrow spaces of the hallway as if to encourage an urgency in those she tries to contact. When she trips over one of many obstacles littering the floor, she kicks out in fury and hurls a bag down the hall like a football. Something smashes out of sight in the shadows.

Phone pressed to her ear, she listens to Morag's interminable recorded message for the third time in as many minutes. 'Ain't here. Say somefing nice.'

'Morag. Me again. I'm in a real bind. Can you please, please come in early. It's my little girl. She's had an accident at school.' As if determined to smash her index finger through the phone screen, Jess ends the call and activates another. One hand on her forehead, her other fist clamps the handset to an ear as if adding force to her skull will push out the pressure within.

Haloed by the dazzling light pouring into the rear of the house, Flo is reduced to little more than a blackened silhouette within the living room, bent forward in a wheelchair. But, as if drawn to the sound of her carer's distress in the hallway, her tatty head turns upon its withered neck. From the distant garden, a commotion begins among the birds.

Too preoccupied to notice Flo's scrutiny, or the agitation from the garden, Jess rests her forehead against the inside of the front door. Supporting her weight with her head she appears to bow into the darkness that pools below the stained-glass wheel above her.

'Penny! Thank Christ! Can't get no one to answer their bloody phone today. But love, can you get up Izzy's school? She's had an accident. They just rang. I can't get cover. Stuck here till six.'

Beyond the living room, the bird cries grow to a cacophony.

Into Jess's ear pours the first smidgen of good news she's heard all day. 'Of course, my love. I was going that way for school pickups. I'll leave now.'

Jess tears up but keeps emotion out of her voice. 'Thanks, Pen. Thank you, thank you. Lifesaver. I'll make it up.'

Through the open door to the living room, Flo continues to watch her carer. Or rather to study Jess, who hangs up, turns from the door and gingerly picks her way through the obstacles on the hall floor. Heading for the living room, she dabs her eyes, sniffs and composes herself, attempting a transformation from frantic mother to professional, dutiful carer.

Reaching the wheelchair, she releases the brake and pushes Flo out of the dim, stuffy room. She rolls her across the patio, down the ramp and into the sunny garden. At each rotation of the wheels, Flo's expression grows alert, her eyes keener.

'Things gotta change, my love,' Jess says. 'This can't go on. None of it. For you an' all. This place ain't healthy. Not right. Not for you. But Jess ain't leaving you to the dark. In our time together, there's going to be loads more fresh air, light, exercise. Maybe even music. What do you say?'

'Shut your fucking mouth.'

Jess stops. Though better prepared now for this kind of response from her client, it's a familiarity with the verbal abuse that brings her to a standstill. 'Where'd you . . .' Jess disregards her own query and pushes the wheelchair further across the lawn in the direction of the grove. 'That's not very nice, Flo. I'm not your enemy, love. I'm here to be your friend. If you'll let me. So why don't you tell me about these beautiful flowers. You choose them?'

'Shouldn't be here.'

'I wish I knew the names of trees too. I love them but couldn't tell you what any of them are called. Bet you could tell me.'

'You're not fit to be a mother.'

This time Jess stops with a finality that suggests the wheelchair will not advance one inch further across the lawn. Her patience with the woman in the wheelchair ends in a heartbeat. A nerve has not merely been touched but stamped upon. The noises of the distressed birds rise as Jess's surprise melts into rage.

'Out! Bitch!' This, barked from the hunched figure sat in the wheelchair.

White with anger, Jess snatches her hands from the chair's handles as if they glow red. And she's running to the house, abandoning Flo on the lawn. The bird cries grow to a din, hastening if not chasing her out of the garden.

Inside the living room, Jess rips at the remaining skin above her cuticles and retreats deeper inside the unlit, cluttered house. One side of her face swells. Her client's brittle words flourish inside her mind. They cackle, loop, repeat. Words she's heard before.

Jess sinks into the musty sinus of the vicarage and feels herself reduced to no more than a shadow upon the threshold of the living room. As if possessing reaching fingers, the landfill of the hall scrapes her ankles and she vanishes more than withdraws to where the fanlight's vivid rays do not reach. Where darkness cloaks her.

Outside, in the distance, Flo talks kindly as if a child stands before her chair. Or maybe she speaks to the birds with the clear expectation that they might be listening.

From the dimmest portion of the hall, gloved by shadows that torrent from the staircase, Jess can only hear Flo's voice but not what she is saying. Nor does she want to. Nor will she look at that frail tyrant. Not for a while.

12

*L*eaning over the banister, Jess can see Flo, sleeping in the living room. Head down, lipless mouth closed, the wheelchair stricken by the afternoon light blasting through the open windows. A breeze stirs the nets and ruffles papers somewhere out of sight.

Jess continues up the stairs, passing the wheelchair's stair-lift, stepping like a goat on a mountain pass to navigate a frozen avalanche of bags and boxes. After stealthily crossing the barricade she reaches the summit for the first time and can only look aghast at the disorder of the first floor.

As on the ground floor, up here a poorly-lit exhibition of antiquities with no curator is strewn, piled and propped. A jumbled archive of a long life bereft of a librarian. 'Bloody tip.'

Before wandering far, she pauses to examine the rusting blade of an ancient scythe mounted upon a wall. A brutal and grotesque agricultural artefact, and her distaste only increases when she investigates the line drawing hanging opposite the scythe. An original illustration made indistinct by a thick layer of dust and the impoverished light. But she can make out a cart being hauled through woodland by a hunched figure. Not a horse but a man. A second figure, one even more indistinct beneath the dross of the ages that films everything up here, follows the cart. The vehicle contains a large spherical shape.

Mystified, Jess moves off and pauses outside Flo's bedroom. The door has been left wide open and a rectangle of daylight promises instant relief from the unpleasant claustrophobic darkness of the landing. She doesn't hesitate and pads inside.

Despite the confusion and gloom of the vicarage encroaching right up to the threshold of this door, Flo's bedroom is striking in its neatness. Old-fashioned elegance and tasteful furnishings encourage Jess to tread carefully and self-consciously to the largest window, which she promptly throws wide open.

From up here, the furthest border of the property is absorbed by the copse of tall trees, their shadows blackening the air between the trunks, but not completely concealing a shimmer of water at the heart of the glade. The hallowed atmosphere she intuited earlier continues to cling to the wooded area.

Drawn to the multitude of framed black-and-white photographs on the dresser opposite the foot of the bed, Jess puts aside her fascination with the grove and, as if nervous of being caught in the room, approaches the pictures on light feet to lessen the creaks of the old floorboards.

One photograph catches her interest immediately, of an elegant younger woman she assumes is Flo, flanked by a pretty little girl and a formally dressed older boy.

Jess glances about the other tastefully framed photographs and quickly deduces that this is a shrine to a happy mother and her two children who once lived at the vicarage. Their apparel suggests the 1960s to the early '70s.

No father is visible anywhere. The little girl, however, appears to occupy centre stage in every photograph. A beautiful and bashful but ever-smiling girl, captured here from infancy to around the age of twelve. In contrast, her older brother appears dour and self-absorbed. Of him there are fewer pictures, and, as with his sister, nothing of him beyond his juvenile years.

BANG. BANG. BANG.

Like gunshots, furious crashes from downstairs pierce the silence of Nerthus House. Doors being slammed. Quickly followed by the noise of utensils dropping and scattering upon a hard floor.

Jess turns and races from the bedroom. Breathless, and precipitating a landslide of plastic bags upon the stairs, she bolts through the house to reach the living room. Only to find Flo sat in her chair awake but merely staring at the blank television screen.

Jess runs from the living room, crosses the hall and inspects the kitchen.

Her ransacked shoulder bag lies upside down on the floor, her personal belongings scattered to the four corners of the room. Bewildered, she gapes at the mess at her feet, then briefly peers at the three cupboard doors that hang open.

By the time she's back inside the living room, she's breathing hard to steady her nerves and control her voice. 'Flo. You . . . My bag?'

Flo ignores Jess but begins to rock back and forth while staring at the dead television screen.

Jess returns to the kitchen, falls to her knees and begins gathering her scattered possessions before throwing them into her bag.

SCRAPE.

At the sounds of a key thrust into the front door lock, she flinches and clutches at her heart. 'Christ alive!'

Morag's entrance into the vicarage is as abrupt as it is noisy. Without a glance at Jess, the night worker bustles into the hall. 'Barely had a wink of sleep. You owe me big time.'

Before the woman can unzip her quilted coat, Jess is in her face, her words taut with suppressed anger. 'You think it's funny?'

'What you on about?'

'Give you pleasure, does it? Have a laugh, did you?'

'Eh?'

'Keeping me in the bloody dark. There's nothing in the notes about . . . Any surprise she's so bloody disturbed with all the curtains shut?'

'You ain't fillin' me with much confidence, if this is how you is first day.'

'Bloody cheek!'

'What else she done?'

'Threw her lunch all over the floor for starters. And spat in my bloody face! In the garden, she . . .'

Morag performs a poor show of stifling laughter. 'She don't eat nothing but biscuits and kippers.'

'There, that! What kind of diet is that?'

'What she likes.'

'She ain't right. And what she said in the garden. She's knocked off! This whole place . . . it's . . .'

Ignoring Jess, Morag thumps past her and glances into the living room. 'All right, Blossom!'

Upon seeing the clean surfaces and washed dishes inside the kitchen, the night worker raises her chin and snorts. A condition of order and cleanliness she sets about destroying by throwing down a carrier bag bulging with shopping. Following the disdainful, entitled dumping of the contents of the supermarket bag upon the counters, Morag tosses down her rucksack, phone and a new magazine and reclaims her territory.

Before following Morag into the kitchen, Jess looks nervously in the direction of the living room. From this angle, with the afternoon light searing the broad windows at the back, she can't be certain which way Flo is looking, whether at her or into the garden.

From the kitchen, Morag gleefully adds insult to injury. 'I told you she don't like no one going outside with her.'

Jess crowds the older woman. 'No, you bloody didn't.'

Morag turns aside to avoid Jess's glare. 'Didn't I?'

Jess jabs a pointed finger at the front door. 'No! Cus you was too busy running through that bloody door this morning to tell me anything useful. How often's she taken outside?'

'You take her out and leave her. Or else you know about it! Then she's away with the fairies, happy.'

'She's abusive. Violent.'

'Dementia with Lewy bodies ain't no picnic for no one.'

Jess checks herself, then the time, snatches up her bag and races from the kitchen. In the hallway, she looks once more at Flo, sitting motionless in the living room. It's still too hard to determine the position of the client's head. 'Bye, Flo.'

Flo doesn't twitch.

From the kitchen doorway, hardly concealing a smirk at Flo's rejection, Morag watches Jess let herself out. As she turns the bulk of her body to the fridge she issues a final contribution to the shift handover. 'Don't forget you's on nights tomorrow. Sheila's sent you a text.'

When the front door closes behind Jess and she escapes the dark chaos of Flo's maze-like home, sunlight explodes upon her face, startling her. She gulps at the fresh air as if breaking from cold, black water. Stepping out from under the porch canopy and into the enchanted idyll of Eadric village, she shields her eyes and notices the elderly woman across the lane. She's standing in her front garden, watching Jess. The woman remains as silent and still as a mime or statue. A tall, angular figure wearing a wide-brimmed sun hat. It's the grandmother Jess saw bidding goodbye to her beautiful family earlier. Glimmering through the shadow of the hat's brim, exposed teeth shape an unpleasant grin.

Two other female faces, sunken and creased by age, peer from the windows of their homes on the lane, their pale flesh ghostly behind grey nets.

When Jess turns to confront the watchers, she might have released a pause function on a remote-control handset.

The activity of the gardener resumes and she busies herself behind a symmetrical hedge with whatever task she'd paused when Jess came through the front door of the vicarage. The pair of thin faces at the windows dissolve into the gloom they recently prodded out of.

Behind her, the front door is yanked open and Morag roars, 'Where's my bloody chicken!'

Jess doesn't break her stride, or even look back at Nerthus House.

13

*T*he subsonic pulse of dance music throbs from the flat above. Beneath a ceiling that suggests it might be quivering like a drum skin, Jess looks up from the slip of paper she's struggling to make sense of. A school accident report.

Penny, her child-minder, stands beside her with her arms folded tightly, her expression tense.

Leaning against the kitchen counter beside the stove, Tony stands and peers at his feet: the very picture of a concerned crestfallen father.

Jess directs all of her attention at Penny. 'They said another child on the phone. This says children were involved. Children. An altercation. She been attacked?'

Breaking Jess's encirclement, Penny looks to Tony and exchanges glances with him. 'Tone saw the head, luv.'

When Tony finally catches Jess's eye he appears sheepish, if not a little guilty at being fingered as the saviour. 'School called me cus you couldn't get away. I was right in the middle of a service an' all. I took off so fast, fellas at work thought I found a bomb under the bonnet.' He laughs and Penny smiles. Jess's face doesn't twitch.

Tony kills his grin. 'Three girls. Not the first time they've gone for her neither. Apparently. I was shocked to hear it. Afraid I tore a strip off that head teacher for not dealing with it better first time.'

His remarks wither Jess with a shame she smothers by turning away from them and leaving the kitchen.

After her own exhausting day, the youngest member of this small family is already asleep. Izzy's small battered shoes lie beside her bed. A toy and comfort muslin are tucked under the little girl's grazed chin and top lip.

At the sight of the abrasion, Jess gasps and instinctively touches the scar on her own mouth. Her face crumples but she stifles her distress when her daughter stirs.

Jess picks up the pink spiral-bound notebook that Izzy keeps on the side table, beside a night-light and a collection of small unicorns who have been put to bed, tucked inside socks. Izzy draws in this book and has been using it today. She's left the book open.

Jess checks the most recent additions and identifies a character with hair resembling Izzy's bunches, embellished with a pink bow. She's a cartoon girl who has been pushed to the floor and hurt her head. Another crudely drawn girl, with fierce black eyes, issues a speech bubble: 'You wear riffy shoes.' A second female tormentor chants, 'Smelly Belly, Smelly Belly.'

Jess replaces the book and leaves her daughter's room as if she cannot bear to be in the same space as the drawing.

Penny holds Jess and does what she can to comfort her. Around her strangled sobs, Jess can just about get her words out. 'She didn't even see her mum before bedtime.'

'You can't always be there, love.'

Tony chips in. 'Problem with shifts, Jess.'

At the sound of his voice, Jess pulls away from Penny and stalks to her shoulder bag. Without looking at Tony, who's eager to take part in the conversation, Jess withdraws her purse and takes out a twenty-pound note.

Penny shakes her head. 'Put it away, Jess. Tone was there before me. He brought her home, put her to bed. I did nothing. Just wanted to see you was okay.'

'You helped.'

'I ain't taking it.'

Jess looks to the ceiling, tearful, beseeching.

Penny comes to her and slips an arm around her shoulder, rests her head on Jess's.

Tony sidles over too, exchanging a sympathetic but concerned glance with Penny. He carefully places a hand between Jess's shoulders. But before he gets far with rubbing her back, Jess stiffens and slips away.

He's left embarrassed and Penny shifts uncomfortably, unable to look at much besides the floor. A tense silence transforms the room into a still life, featuring three subjects who won't look at each other.

'I better get off,' Penny says and makes for her coat.

Jess follows her to the door and into the small reception. Once out of Tony's earshot she clutches Penny's arm. 'Pen. Tomorrow night. They want me to work. Can you take Izz?'

'I can't, love. Sorry. I got Helen's twins already.'

'No worries. Later, yeah. And thanks for today.'

The women briefly hug before Penny opens the door.

Jess dabs at her eyes and warily returns to the kitchen, straightening her spine to restore the composure she resents abandoning.

'I can stay for a bit, Jess.'

The front door closes and Jess looks in that direction as if surprised to hear the door, or to avoid Tony's eyes. 'No. No, thanks. Thanks for helping. An' everything. But . . . You know. The terms.'

'Look. I'm earning good money now, Jess. Nights? They're no good for Izzy. I can finally get us . . . Get both of you out of this shit-tip.' He moves towards her again, his face a mask of sympathy, his arms shaping an embrace he hopes she'll accept.

Without meeting his eye once, Jess steps away and bumps the little table as she retreats to the door. 'No. Thank you. I'll be there next time. Won't happen again.'

'You just call. Any time. For anything at all. I'll always be there for both of you.'

Jess nods an uncomfortable acknowledgement but keeps her face turned to the side when alone with him. 'Gotta check on Izz, yeah?' She turns awkwardly and hurries from the room.

14

The following night.

*T*he sun sets behind Nerthus House as Jess marches towards it, tugging Izzy behind her. Before the stone edifice thrusting at the sky, the small family of two diminishes and grows less distinct within the long shadows. Izzy is additionally dwarfed by a stuffed backpack and carries a panda bear under her arm. Jess is loaded down with plastic carrier bags and a holdall. Amongst the magnificent homes and splendid gardens of Eadric, they could be mistaken for refugees.

As they slow to a dawdle on the front path, Izzy gapes at the daunting, mysterious old house where she's going to spend the night. 'I want to stay with Daddy.'

'Izz! Been through it. Ain't going through it again. So stop.'

But it doesn't take Izzy long to enliven with surprise and curiosity before the floral arrangements erupting from the front garden of the vicarage. The prospect of adventure lures her onto the grass and she prances across the front lawn, swinging her toy panda. She sets herself for a handstand but fails. Her attempt clumsy, all pushed-out bum and flailing legs.

Before Jess can rummage out the keys from her bag the front door is yanked open from within. Jess and Izzy jump.

51

Morag barrels out and thumps into the porch, glaring at the relief. Eyeing the little girl with specific displeasure, she bites down on launching into a tirade. Izzy responds with a serious expression and thrusts out her panda, its limbs flopping. 'This is Nurse Bamboo. She looks after old people.'

Jess pushes a hand down through the air to calm her daughter. 'Not now, love.'

After raising an eyebrow at Izzy's declaration of intent, Morag returns her glare to the girl's mother. But Jess holds her head high. 'Couldn't get childcare. It's just for the night.' She turns to Izzy and motions for her to stay put on the lawn, then ushers Morag to a place on the path where they can stand out of earshot. Accepting the exclusion, Izzy happily flies her panda round the front garden of the vicarage. 'Bamboo's bringing in the medicine!'

Morag's angry stare bores into Jess. 'Blossom ain't slept a wink last night. Or moved, or said nothing all day. Don't know what you done to her yesterday. And your kid ain't covered by company insurance. Blossom don't want her mooching froo her fings neither.'

'She won't. She knows—'

Morag brushes past Jess and trundles down the path. When she makes the pavement she turns and bellows, 'And don't touch nothing in the fridge with my name on it! Blossom'll have your face off, you ever give her chicken again. And I will if it's mine.'

Bewildered by Morag's raised voice, Izzy watches her waddle off. She looks to her mum, her panda drooping from one hand. 'Mummy got told off.'

'Come on, love. Let's start the sleep-over, yeah?'

In silence, Izzy rushes to join her mum who ushers her into the gaping black mouth of the vicarage before closing the front door behind them.

Inside the reception, the light dims and the inner gloom claims them.

15

As ever, Flo's rheumy eyes are glazed yet enthralled with what lies either beyond the open French windows or within her dwindling mind.

Jess switches off the television. A programme Morag was watching. 'Bet that's been on all day. Surprised it ain't caught fire.' Warily she approaches the wheelchair. 'You ain't in a draught there, my love?'

Equal parts fascinated and horrified at such an aged spectacle, Izzy follows her mother. When Jess notices her daughter's passage towards the wheelchair, she extends an arm, preventing Izzy from getting too close. 'Remember what I said? She don't know you and she gets upset. You don't go near her chair. Ever. At all. Yeah?'

Izzy nods her assent and Jess turns to Flo. 'This is my daughter. Izzy. She'll be here tonight with us. Gonna be a right girls' night in.'

Jess winks at Izzy then kneels before her wizened ward. As she adjusts Flo's gown and spreads a blanket across her lap, her actions are more akin to defusing a bomb than attending to a dementia patient. When Jess attempts to delicately wipe Flo's mouth with a warm flannel her ministrations grow more nervy. Moments after she begins dabbing the wash-cloth on her client's chin, she hesitates.

Flo's face has been transformed by a smile. And this is no ordinary smile. It is one of intense joy. The old woman's milky eyes have even moistened as she stares in wonder and adoration at Izzy.

Jess looks at her daughter, who's come to stand beside the chair and now bashfully returns the old woman's smile. When Flo extends a lumpy hand towards Izzy, Jess tenses, looks at Izzy and shakes her head firmly. 'No closer.'

Jess rises to her feet and removes Morag's dirty plate, mug and magazines from the nearest armchair. 'Izz. You come and sit here. Do some colouring.'

But Izzy remains entranced by Flo. And while Jess's back is briefly turned, the little girl shuffles closer to Flo and accepts the extended lumpy fingers. 'Your nails are long.'

Bent over, tidying the chair and side table of Morag's mess, Jess is seized with panic and turns. Only to stare in disbelief at the sight of her daughter and Flo, who not only smile at each other, like two children at a birthday party, but are now holding hands.

Swallowing the constriction in her throat, Jess whispers, 'Izzy.'

Izzy lets go of Flo's hand, which remains in the air as if pleading for more contact with the child.

'I want to go in the garden,' Izzy says, though she may have been sharing her intention with either of the adults in the room.

Outside, with Bamboo, she proceeds to happily caper about the lawn. Two attempts at handstands are dismal failures. Not even close.

'Stay where I can see you!' With a weary sigh, Jess slumps into the space she's cleared on the armchair beside Flo's wheelchair. And in silence, side by side, both women are lost to their preoccupations. Flo stares at Izzy racing around the lawn as if she's watching a miracle from heaven unfold before her aged eyes. Jess stares at her sore cuticles and bitten-down nails.

16

From the lane before the vicarage any regular observer would notice how proud Nerthus House seems to have awoken. And how it now appears to smile, though grimly, in a line of lit windows at the front, ground floor. The expression beams from out of a dark, weathered face with its eyes closed, or missing. And, for the first time in years, the new lights of the hall and kitchen cast out a rainbow. A powerful illumination projected through the stained glass wheel above the front door.

Moving a small set of steps under the cobwebbed, fly-specked fittings, Jess has spent the first part of the evening changing the bulbs of the vicarage's ground floor. Incrementally, and with some satisfaction, she's able to survey how she has dispelled the gloom and shadows from some of the dusty rat-runs in Flo's neglected home. The disarray of the reception and staircase is now floodlit by fresh bulbs. From the dining room a white luminance pours. From the living room, more light bursts from the walls and ceiling.

When she takes another look into the tatty living room, Flo's chair remains in position facing Izzy, who sits out of arm's reach as she's been bidden and is still happily chattering and raising her drawing pad to show Flo what she's created.

'There's three unicorns. The mummy one is pink. Children are blue and green.'

Flo rocks gently and beams at Izzy until her regal laugh charms the living room. A refined trill, the amusement and delight genuine.

Not even Jess can resist a rare smile tonight. More reassured that Izzy is not in danger and can be trusted, she slips to the stairs, carrying her small stepladder and calling out another warning as she moves. 'Don't get no closer, Izz.'

'I won't.'

After refreshing the first bulb on the landing, Jess steps down from the ladder to better see the curious line drawing that she glanced at yesterday. Under better light it draws the eye.

Using a duster she wipes away the film of dross and unveils a detailed depiction of a small lake or pond that shines beneath a full moon. Along a straight track, a wooden cart is pulled towards the water by a hunched and dishevelled beggar with one hand. The other extremity ends in a dark, gruesome stump. Now that more of the illustration is exposed, she can see also that the abject figure's head is turned and an appalling face with black, empty eye sockets is revealed. The tatty figure is blind and has been tasked with towing the large sphere inside the cart. A vessel that appears to have been constructed intricately with hawthorn sticks.

A naked woman follows the cart, holding a scythe. Her face is obscured by a cascade of straight hair and a tiara woven from flowers and briar. A maiden, youthful and lithe, her shoulders proudly thrown back as if with resolve or purpose. And towards the pond they go, and from the black water a powerful light leaps.

At the furthest edge of the pond's dark surface rises a suggestion of a third figure. This one is too long and thin to be human and appears as a black silhouette more than a fully rendered form. It partially blends into the surrounding trees and stands knee-deep in the murky water. Into where the moonlight shafts from on high, it extends two spindly arms, the limbs fashioned from sticks.

A human female shape is also suggested by the body of the thing in the pool, though the height of the form would be several times that of a woman. Other than these details, the bulk of the inky silhouette remains indistinct save for a cruel beak, jutting from the creature's sleek head and the surrounding shadow that capes the rear of the water. Perhaps with some sense of expectation, or eagerness, even greed, the entity watches the progression of the cart as it draws nearer to the water.

Bemused, Jess wipes more dust from the bottom of the glass and squints to read the curving script at the foot of the picture: 'Mother. Creator. Destroyer.'

She pulls a face and turns away only to have her vision snag upon the rusted scythe, wall-mounted, across the landing. Averting her eyes, she shakes loose the keys on the old brass ring shaped like the sun. And tries a key in the lock of the closed bedroom door next to Flo's master bedroom.

No good.

Another key.

No good.

But the third key delivers a satisfying CLUNK inside the lock.

Once the door is open and a smear of light falls into the murky half-lit space, Jess appears ready to step into an old photograph more than a dim, brownish room. The furniture, and every item upon the walls and shelves and bookcases, remains in a pristine arrangement.

Jess goes inside and unscrews the dead bulb from the ceiling shade. She replaces it with a new bulb from her pocket and returns to the chunky Bakelite light switch.

The refreshed ceiling light shines on a veritable time capsule of a girl's bedroom, perfectly preserved from the 1970s, equipped with a record player, a Bay City Rollers poster, another of Gary Glitter and Alvin Stardust, a crochet blanket, a transistor radio, yellow, brown and orange wallpaper, posters from magazines taped onto the wardrobe. And all of it lightly peppered with dust. But the room is not that dirty, as if it was cleaned until recently.

In places, relics from an even older childhood are visible. A doll house, a stack of antique board games, stuffed toys. A stratum of an even younger girl's existence, its place in history preserved. All part of a life captured in this evidence of its amusements and fascinations, maintained for decades then sealed away.

Jess bends to read the name on the array of gymnastics medals and certificates arranged around the mirror of an antique dressing table. *Charlotte Gardner.* On all of them.

'Your little girl.'

After carefully descending the stairs and sliding around the newel post in the hall, Jess pulls up in surprise. Then readies herself to race into the living room on red alert.

She changes her mind and remains still, silent and watchful. At a distance, without Flo and Izzy knowing, Jess observes the interaction in the living room.

Izzy now kneels before the footplates of Flo's wheelchair within easy reach of those old hands, still so capable of swiping fast. Head down, Izzy sketches furiously while nodding her head as if receiving instructions. Flo is leaning forward and smiling sweetly. But also whispering, though her frail voice is too low for Jess to make out words at this distance.

Before Flo's eager face, Izzy briefly pauses her sketching to draw a small imaginary circle in the air. 'Like that? No. Even bigger!' Izzy fashions a much bigger circle before her face with her fingers. Together, in perfect synchronicity, Flo and Izzy criss-cross the air-wheel with spokes, giggling once the action is complete. Gently, Flo then extends one withered hand and touches the graze on Izzy's face.

Which breaks Jess from her trance. She races into the living room and as she moves she hears Izzy say, 'Mean girls done it.'

17

Silent. Morose. Flo. Illumined by silver moonlight. Her small form a crease in the middle of the vast bed. The tiny head propped up amidst plump pillows. Her craggy face turned to the windows, eyes still pining for the garden.

Beside the bed, an easy chair and a side table. Upon the latter the estate agent's brochure is smoothed out beside Jess's bag, her phone and a cup of steaming coffee. Only the lambent moon of a small lamp, with the shade angled down, offers light.

Jess stands beside the chair and taps the headrest. 'I'll be right here all night, Flo. Just gonna tuck Izzy in.'

Cowering inside a sleeping bag laid on top of the vintage bed in Charlotte Gardner's room, Izzy's wide eyes peer over the head of Bamboo, the panda that she clutches beneath her chin. The moment her mother appears in the doorframe, Izzy beseeches her to adjust the sleeping arrangements. 'Don't like it here. Can I sleep with Mummy and Flo?'

Jess pads across the room, sits on the bed and strokes her daughter's hair. 'Baby girl. Just an old house. All it is.'

At the merest contact from her mother's hand, Izzy seizes Jess's waist as if Mum is buoyant wreckage in a terrifying black sea. 'There's . . . shapes. I heard . . . moving.'

'Mmm? This was another little girl's room once. Just a happy girl who left it full of sweet dreams.'

Izzy isn't convinced.

'I gotta keep an eye on Flo, my love. Old people don't sleep very well and I don't want her waking you up all night. But I'll be in here every ten minutes to check on you.'

'Five minutes . . . Three.'

'Promise. And I ain't going until you're asleep.' Jess kisses her daughter's head. Izzy fights tears. Jess's eyes drift to the sketch pad and felt-tip pens on the dresser beside the bed.

Izzy's latest picture features three girls with red faces, running in the foreground of what appears to be a wood. Their mouths are wide and howling, their arms claw for safety. Behind them, a thin form like a stretched person rises tall. A starved thing, inked black, with a water-bird's beak stabbing outwards from a slender head. The creature's feet are concealed by the circular body of water, maybe a pond, from which it emerges. About the scene another circle forms a halo as bright as a sun.

Glancing over her shoulder, through the thin light of the lamp, Jess confirms that Flo sleeps. The frail figure is lying perfectly still beneath the luxurious eiderdown. Satisfied, Jess leaves the room.

On the first-floor landing, she rotates another old key and unlocks a second bedroom. Then fishes a bulb out of her pocket and slips inside the dark room.

With the ceiling light refreshed, for the second time that evening she stands amazed. Her upturned face takes in a squadron of kit-set military aircraft, dusty but artfully assembled and painted, all hanging from the ceiling. Scores of them. Turning about, she surveys more of a space made orderly with a military precision. The walls are filled with photographs and detailed line drawings of RAF aircraft, from the Second World War to the jets of the 1970s. A bed that would pass muster in a barracks fits neatly against one wall. The contents atop the small desk are as neat as the boy must have been when he occupied the room decades hence. A butterfly collection and a library of well-looked-after books and annuals from a younger world are all coated with dust, though lightly. As with the girl's room, the area has been maintained until recently.

Upon the desk, a photograph features the boy from the family portraits in Flo's room. He's wearing an air cadet uniform and receiving an award from a smiling adult officer. That very certificate, awarded to a Phillip Gardner in 1978, remains tacked beside the photograph.

Becoming uncomfortable within a room as cold and clinical as a cell for a military obsessive, Jess withdraws and turns off the light as she leaves.

Carefully opening the top drawer of the dresser in Flo's bedroom, Jess's eyes immediately find two transparent sachets containing locks of hair – blonde and black. They are dated: *Charlotte, 1972. Phillip, 1972.* Stacked wallets of photographs form a dais beneath the sachets of hair.

Jess raises and leafs through the top wallet, her attention gripped by the very first picture, in which a much younger Flo sits beside her little girl, Charlotte. The two of them flank a record player in the vicarage lounge, a room captured in better days.

The remaining pictures in the envelope feature Flo with the sombre, awkward Phillip and beaming Charlotte.

The Vessel

Somewhere in the Mediterranean. Holiday snaps.

Jess rummages deeper inside the drawer and withdraws a second wallet from near the bottom of the pile. These photographs are also old but their vintage is more recent than the preceding family portraits.

Behind her back, without so much of a creak of a bedspring, Flo spreads her arms and pulls herself upright.

Jess is engrossed with the photograph she has selected and withdrawn from the deck. A sun-blanched picture, the tones diluted orange, that features a group of women of varying ages, half a dozen, some elderly, who are seated on blankets around a pond in a wooded grove. It might be a picture of a study group, or a women's group. The arrangement suggests a self-help ensemble.

Flo is in the picture. She sits at the side of the group, which listens to a much older woman at the head of the pond who has taken advantage of the shade. Flo is older here too, her hair longer, her face drawn and unsmiling. And yet she's still glamorous in middle age and dressed fashionably for the '70s.

The other pictures in the wallet continue the theme of the first photograph. Sun-blanched portraits of the summer idyll that once existed in the vicarage garden, decades before. The same women, with only a few additions, appear in each picture. All appear happy, some are laughing, some hold hands, some wear floral tiaras. As a group they repeatedly appear arranged in a rough, informal ring on the lawn, in which they partake of a kind of sisterly celebration. In one scene, a trestle table is loaded with fruit, bread, cakes, wine. In several other snapshots, two women kneel in the centre of the ring and appear to be constructing some form of wheel, or wreath, from sticks entwined with bright flowers. In several other photographs a kind of dome rises in the background; half a sphere woven out of hawthorn.

63

All of the women appear ordinary. Mums, daughters, grandmothers, neighbours perhaps. But the wheel and odd creel add a subtle pagan touch to the enigmatic gatherings.

In each ensemble, the only woman permanently without a smile or a sun-browned face, who rears proud but pale and unhappy at the side of the gatherings, is Flo. Often she sits beside the elderly woman who was addressing the group in the first picture at the pond. The matron repeatedly holds Flo's elegant white hand as if offering motherly reassurance at a difficult time.

Jess returns the photographs to the wallets and neatens the stack before easing the drawer closed.

Behind her, Flo silently lowers herself to her pillows.

Her mooching over, Jess turns about and tiptoes to her armchair to begin the vigil of the night carer.

Inside the room next door and within the old bed, Izzy sleeps. Her arms tightly hug her panda. Her forehead glistens with sweat and her lips work at unspoken words.

In the armchair beside Flo's bed, Jess has succumbed to the sleep of the exhausted. Beyond the orderly bedroom, beyond the dim sepia rectangle of the open door, the vast house breathes quietly.

While Jess sleeps deeply, her head on one side, mouth slightly open and body slumped into the armchair, her client lies embedded within plump cushions. With her eyes open.

Outside the vicarage the oceanic sounds of a great surging begin within the woods, growing until the nocturnal wind thrashes the mighty, ancient trees.

Flo sits up in bed. An emaciated figure, her thinning hair wild. She stares at the door as if alert to a summons. And begins a gentle rocking, back and forth.

Jess frowns, stirs and nearly rouses but doesn't wake. She sinks away instead into much needed rest, her face blank, near lifeless. Bound by fatigue, she is not alert to the rustle in the room. That passes onto the landing. Nor does she pay heed to the gentle bumps of someone who is on all fours outside the room and crawling through the dark.

Instead Jess dreams of the vicarage garden blackened by night. At the bottom of the lawn, great trees protect the glade – a mighty stockade that thrusts at a night sky dizzy with stars. A moon, so vast that it appears to be a new planet, presses the earth's atmosphere. The tumult of the urgent wind grows. It roars and crashes amidst the primaeval woodland that extends forever; the spaces between the mighty legs of the trees, lightless fathoms of pitch. Threading through the turmoil, the bony notes of a woodwind instrument rise and fall, as if prospecting or searching.

Izzy runs out from the vicarage and performs a series of perfect cartwheels across the shorn grass.

Behind her, like an excitable dog scampering after its mistress, an old figure dressed in a pale nightgown capers swiftly on all fours. Flo. Together they bound to the border of the grove where old Flo rears on to her hind legs before the tree-line.

Izzy comes to a standstill beside her and together they face the moon-bathed glade. Facing the trees as if in wondrous subjugation to them, Izzy and Flo draw an identical but invisible wheel shape in the air in perfect synchronicity, their hands moving in an anticlockwise direction. In the middle of their imaginary circles they cross the spokes at exactly the same time and speed.

The sound of the mighty night wind rises to a critical mass and is dragged backwards like a spring tide pulled by a new moon. A whirlpool of violent air that retreats then gushes about the wood anticlockwise.

The faint piping rises through the scales and heralds the emergence of a large form surfacing from still water, somewhere nearby but hidden inside the trees. In response to whatever moves about that dark water, Flo and Izzy throw their arms wider, their palms upturned. Grinning, they both slowly rise from the earth and into thin air, lingering a few metres from the ground.

Before them, the tops of the trees sway then part as if to allow access to a vast shape.

Jess wakes suddenly, her sleep broken by a distant, urgent, repetitive trill. A ringtone. Her phone is ringing somewhere in the distance of the vicarage.

Turning her bleary face, she gapes at the side table where her phone should be. There lies a mug of cold coffee and the estate agent's brochure. But no phone.

In panic, Jess clutches at her cheeks as if to claw sleep, and what it made her imagine, from her skull. Disorientated and struggling to make sense of where she is and what's happening around her, she turns to face the doorway and the distant sound of her phone.

Beside her, Flo sleeps peacefully.

Jess is out of her chair as if electrocuted. Stumbling on sleep-sedated legs, she weaves to the bedroom door.

Jess turns away from the sight of Izzy safely asleep in Charlotte Gardner's old bedroom and focuses on where the phone's ringtone cries out. From below.

Downstairs.

The realisation of such an impossibility leaves her swaying on the landing below the rusty sickle as if still asleep.

Forcing herself to descend the staircase, she pads into darkness.

In what ambient light seeps here, from the night-lights of the two bedrooms, the murk of the lower floor transforms Flo's detritus into ominously indistinct humps and heads and silhouettes. Everything appears marginally animated. The dark energy of night suggests myriad presences. Flo's enigmatic past crowds her, watching her every footfall through the vicarage.

Jess slaps on the hall light as if her life depends upon it and breathes normally again, unaware she's been holding her breath on the stairs.

The ringtone rises insistent, louder, from somewhere in the murky lower confines of this cavernous building. Pursuing the phone's growing trill, she picks her way about the obstacles on the hallway floor and closes on the dining room. The ringtone is definitely and inexplicably issuing from the midst of the landfill in this room.

Jess turns on the dining room light and edges along a faint dusty track of carpeted floor. She lowers herself to her hands and knees and peers into the black mouth of a tunnel fashioned into the disorder that is piled upon and around the vast dining table. At the mouth of the burrow, Jess reads the post-it note stuck to a box. *Manes exite materni.* And from deep inside this tunnel, the screen of her phone is glowing green and casting a dim light about the boxes, piled garments and the wooden ribs of the chair legs absorbed into the cave's walls.

She goes in. Squeezes herself inside the chute. Around her crawling body the columns of Flo's belongings shift uneasily like the unstable walls of a disused mine shaft. But towards her shrieking handset and along the tunnel she crawls.

On all fours she is soon bumping and panting her way through a narrowing of the fissure, passing objects that remain entirely indistinct. Eventually, when so deeply inside the structure that she could be mistaken for believing she has passed from the room in which the mound exists, she closes upon the glowing handset screen. The insistent scream of the phone vibrates the darkness. At the far end of the passage, where she is forced to duck her head between her shoulders, Jess slows to peer at whatever it is that she has crawled onto.

There is the phone. And lit up by the screen is a strange circular arrangement of odd and unappealing objects. A dirty linen parcel the size of a shoebox, bound with twine. Bird feathers are stuck to the stained fabric. The object has been placed in the centre of a spoked wheel made from sticks.

One she recognises. The pattern resembles the sundial of the stained glass above the front door. And it is the shape that was constructed for the garden celebrations at the vicarage in the '70s.

Around the edge of the twig-wheel, an assortment of curious objects has been placed and abandoned, perhaps years before. A tiny sheaf of wheat. A rustic loaf of desiccated bread. Several small wooden bowls. One bowl contains an oil, another powdered incense.

A grotesque homemade shrine.

Jess empties an age-grimed bowl of dried fennel. The base of the container is inscribed with a wheel-shaped sigil.

She can't bring herself to touch the soiled parcel in the centre of the arrangement. Instead she glances at the phone screen contained inside the wooden wheel. The screen reads: CALLER UNKNOWN.

Jess snatches up the handset and swipes the screen.

'Hello?'

No answer. Only silence.

Jess drops the phone. Down on all fours in the darkness, she bows her head over the dirty shrine. The confining walls press around her head. Trapped by confusion and buried by fear, she doesn't understand what's happening. She's exhausted.

FLAP-CRACK-FLAP!

From out of the darkness next to her face a trapped bird explodes into terrified, frantic life. Jess screams and clutches her face as it is beaten by a flurry of dusty wings.

She ducks. Then forces her body deeper inside the tunnel, scrabbling over the shrine, destroying it as she pushes blindly through what's left of the aperture. She is driven by the slaps and shrieks of the bird behind her and then upon her back. As the terrified creature struggles past her face, the bird's wings beat against her mouth. Its claws tangle in her hair, scrape her scalp like pins. She can stand it no more and bursts up and onto her feet, using the back of her shoulders to force her body upwards and through the first crevice that allows electric light to shaft into this darkness. She rises through a gap between stacked furniture and a grubby window pane – an aperture she enlarges with the upward thrust of her body, disinterring dust-furred and cobwebbed boxes filled with crockery and glass.

Jess snatches at the window latch, her fingers frantic until she thrusts the old window wide. Instantly, her face is buffeted by a shock of cold night air.

The bird noisily rises from her head, the din of its wings bewildering her until it is free.

Grasping her phone to her chest, Jess retreats and stumbles up through the vicarage to the master bedroom. And stops dead at what she is forced to behold.

Withered Flo smiles in her sleep. An old frail woman who hasn't walked in years, who could never clamber out of the vast bed without the same assistance that is required to get her inside it. Nestled against her thin back is little Izzy, sleeping and clutching her panda.

18

*L*ike an evacuee awaiting embarkation, Jess fidgets in the hallway. She checks her watch twice without paying attention to what she reads. The third time she scrapes back a sleeve to seek the correct time, her attention moves no further than Izzy's school bag abandoned on the hall floor.

And sure enough, when she looks down the hall and through the frame of the living room doorway, there is her daughter standing beside Flo's wheelchair. Just enough of the meagre silhouette of her client is visible, dwarfed by the wheelchair. But like two figures in the background of a dark oil painting, a young girl and an elderly woman share an enigmatic fascination that remains a mystery to the onlooker. Whispers pass between them.

'Izz!' Jess calls. When her daughter doesn't respond, she raises her voice. 'Izzy!'

Izzy reluctantly turns her smiling face from Flo to offer her mother a sullen glare. 'Why can't I stay with Flo today?'

'Cus you bloody can't. You got school! How many times I have to tell you?'

At the very mention of that place the resistance in Izzy slumps and she becomes fearful. When she slides a glance at Flo it's as if the elderly dementia patient has just called to her without moving her lips. And as if rapt by the advice of a helpful adult Izzy appears to listen to mute Flo.

Jess tries again. 'Izzy. Come here, please. Now.'

Oblivious to her mother's request, Izzy remains rooted beside Flo and continues to stare into the woman's murky eyes.

SCRAPE. From the other side of the front door, a key angrily buries itself into the lock.

Jess jumps. 'Jesus!'

As soon as Morag has squeezed herself into the vicarage, Jess is in her face. 'She's wandering.'

'Hang on. Ain't got me coat off yet!'

'She took my phone. Last night. My bag yesterday.'

Morag lumbers past Jess. Once she's ambled into the kitchen she unleashes a weary sigh at being back again.

Unseen by Jess as she pursues Morag, intent on making her point, Flo collects one of Izzy's hands and holds it with her own. Izzy giggles then turns her hand up and looks at whatever it is that Flo has placed upon her palm. Secretively, she slips the object into the pocket of her cardigan.

'Don't be bloody stupid,' Morag roars at Jess from inside the kitchen. 'Loss of executive function was three years ago. She ain't taken a step since her stroke. Before I started.'

At the rebuff, Jess zips up her coat angrily.

Morag matches Jess's annoyance by yanking her own zip down. 'You only been here five minutes. What makes you so special? Heal the lame, can you?'

'This place, it . . . ain't right.'

'What you on about?'

'Something happened. Last night.'

'Making no sense. As usual.'

Through the kitchen doorway, Jess glances towards the stairwell. 'Flo has a daughter. A son.'

To be heard above the explosion of a bag's contents that she scatters across the kitchen counters, Morag raises her voice to a familiar bellow. 'I ain't blind! I seen the pictures!'

'And what? Where are they when their mum's like this?'

'Her daughter died when she was little. Sheila said. And her son can't fink much of Blossom. Never been to visit. No letters. Nothin'. Can't say I'm surprised. But nothin' to do with me. Or you.' Morag bustles out of the room and crosses the hall to barge into the living room.

Jess follows as far as the door. From there she can see that Flo has resumed the inexorable rocking back and forth in her chair while whispering to Jess's disobedient, avid, smiling daughter.

'All right, Blossom?' Morag roars on entry.

Flo ignores the greeting and continues to chatter emphatically to Izzy in a hushed voice.

Jess tries again from the doorway. 'Izz!'

Abruptly and as if triggered by the raised voices of her carers, Flo's own voice rises through the octaves. 'Erce! Erce! Erce!'

'Come away, Izz. Now!'

'Erce! Erce! Erce!' Flo cries out again.

Morag is unruffled and casually tosses a comment to Jess. 'She does that sometimes. Means you've disturbed her.'

'Izzy, what did I just ask you to do? Come away. Now!'

Izzy continues to ignore her mother and only stops smiling at Flo to chorus the old woman's cries. 'Erce! Erce! Erce!'

Morag announces self-importantly, 'She was a clever girl, our Blossom. All them languages she could speak. Still does. Bits of them. You can see how many books she's got. Piles. Half ain't in English. Shame it comes to this, though, eh? Don't matter how many books you've read.'

Jess stomps across the room to snatch Izzy's arm and pull her to a safe distance. 'Come away, I said. You deaf? We gotta get going.'

Old Flo watches Izzy being tugged away and sends the girl on her way by shrieking another, 'Erce! Erce! Erce!' Before encoring with, 'Gods cannot be contained inside walls.'

Izzy yanks her arm free of her mother's hand and races back to stand behind Flo's chair. 'I want to help with Flo.'

At first startled, then embarrassed by her daughter's uncharacteristic disobedience, Jess manages to gather herself enough to wither Izzy with a stern look. 'Get here.'

Slowly and sulkily, Izzy stomps to Jess but only to pass by her and head out of the living room.

Delighted by the spectacle, Morag roars with laughter. 'Little Madam! That'll be Blossom's influence!'

Jess follows her sulking daughter to the front door. With her fingers gripping the latch, she hesitates and turns to call to Flo from the hallway. 'Flo. See you tonight.'

Flo doesn't react. Her attention has drifted once more to the garden and the early morning sun that blesses it.

'Bye bye, Flo!' Izzy calls out.

In the distance Flo's head turns swiftly at Izzy's summons. She beams from her chair and waves a twisted hand before using it to trace a circle, clockwise, in the air. This she crosses with invisible spokes. 'Merry meet.'

Jess can only watch dumbfounded and a little hurt. An anguish that only increases when Izzy fashions the same circle in the air and crosses it with spokes. 'Merry part!'

'They's like two peas in a pod!' Morag roars.

With a quick downstroke of her own hand Jess angrily interrupts Izzy's gesticulations, then hurries the recalcitrant girl out the door, one hand applying pressure to her back. A touch that infuriates Izzy enough to shout at her mother, 'Stop pushing!'

19

A dead bird, emaciated and grey, lies upon the shit-spattered cement floor of the abandoned utility room. From the cobweb-encrusted rafters, the thrum of nesting pigeons vibrates the air. Discarded school furniture cowers in corners, veiled in dust and the disused killing funnels of spiders.

Into this distant recess of the primary school, little used and only then for storage, Izzy and an equally timid girl have retreated as far as they are able.

Their instant relief at being concealed is soon tempered by the fearful wonder with which they eye the greening glass of a skylight above them. The grubby panes cast a gloomy underwater glow over the sepulchral space, a stale light extending and bathing their anxious faces.

Izzy approaches an old desk set at a tilt against a broken blackboard and excitedly fans out the colourful trading cards that she clutches in a moist hand. Her friend crowds the table top and begins pointing and speaking around a mouthful of cereal bar. 'Got that. Got that. Got that. And that.'

Once all of the cards are spread out, Izzy smiles into her friend's eyes. 'I got two special editions of Doctor Fizzle. You can have one.'

Her friend's face beams with pleasure but drops just as quickly at something she sees over Izzy's shoulder. 'Izzy.'

They enter the room in silence. Heralding their arrival with an angry commotion would have struck less terror into

Izzy and her friend. The three girls who ransacked Izzy's bag and stole her unicorn form a line blocking the only way out. Today their ranks are reinforced by two boys.

Jess shakes out the duvet over her legs then thumps the pillow into a comfortable shape. The thin curtains of her bedroom are closed but daylight beats through the cheap fabric and stains the room a dull pewter. Above the ceiling, the thump of jungle music, with sub-woofers booming, vibrates the very walls that enclose the bed. In some other place inside the block, a heavy door clashes shut.

Jess lies back and stares at the ceiling. Around her eyes and mouth the strain of the last few days has cast darker shadows and dug deeper lines. A mark from Flo's blow fades upon one cheek. Exhausted enough to cry, she grinds her teeth and slides a sleeping mask over her eyes.

The intruders of the abandoned storeroom crowd Izzy with their grinning triumphant faces. Snatching hands come from either side and from behind her back to seize the trading cards. Some fall to litter the cement floor. The special edition card is tugged from the fingers of her friend. Izzy's cereal bar is plucked from her own hand.

'That a food bank bar?' a girl demands and incites a chorus of shrieked laughter.

'No!' One of the boys roars from the rear. 'Gotta be nice to paupers. Headmistress said!'

Within the torrent of laughter and the raised judgemental voices running interference over each other, Izzy's friend lowers her eyes, then her head, and scurries clear of the scrum, abandoning Izzy.

A second girl, and the thief of her unicorn, has been laughing unkindly but is now furious. 'Knew you was hiding in here. Grass!'

Izzy is pushed hard and falls to her backside.

A sharp communal inhalation of momentarily shocked children sucks at the air in the room, before the space again resounds with laughter.

Izzy makes no attempt to rise, and tears up.

'Chantelle. Don't!' another girl cries out in an unconvincing and half-giggled appeal for restraint.

One of the boys proves he's both quick and aggressive with his hands. He darts in and unclips what will be the second unicorn Izzy's destined to lose from her rucksack within the same week. 'Got it!' he cries before stooping and pinching the fingers of one hand upon the dry wing of the dead bird on the floor. This he tosses at Izzy in exchange for the unicorn. 'Swap ya!'

The bird lands between Izzy's spread ankles with a parched rattle.

Behind the boy, the gang spring back, horrified by the bird's corpse yet more than able to shriek out their mirth.

Izzy's face hardens and her teary eyes narrow. With her bewilderment subsiding, and perhaps because of her unfortunate familiarity with similar situations, she finally summons a glare for her tormentors. Though not for long. Soon, as if distracted by something beyond the room, or as if someone has just called to her from a distance, she raises her face to the grubby skylight and peers intently at the very place from where that long single note originates. A thin sound, as reedy and eerie as those produced by primitive pipes made of bone. It comes to her as faint as a faraway ship's horn or train whistle, softened and made mysterious by the enchantment of distance.

Only she appears to hear the music because only she is staring at the skylight, and growing preoccupied enough to entirely ignore the hostile children. It's as if Izzy now yearns to see who it is who calls to her from afar. No distraction will be permitted to break her expectant vigil. Izzy's hand slips inside the pocket of her cardigan and reappears clutching the small bone carving that Flo gave her that morning. Ancient figurative art depicting a wheel or sun.

'What's Smelly Belly doin'?' the girl who pushed her over asks everyone in the room.

Izzy stands up and closes her eyes.

'Freakin' out,' replies the boy with the unicorn gripped in a sweaty fist.

This statement encourages a chorus of laughter that Izzy appears immune to as she transcribes a anticlockwise circle in the air before her face, the fingers of that very hand clutching the carving. Her lips move and begin to mumble so softly that no one in that room will ever hear what it is that the little girl incants.

Cruel, incredulous laughter explodes from the bullies. At least three of them scream, 'Spaz!'

As if that is a cue, Izzy opens her eyes. With the symbol in her palm, she points up as if to heaven, her little face transformed by beatific wonder. If this is merely a ploy, it is one that she conducts with the silent concentration of a child completely entranced.

In a corner of the room, Izzy's friend is the only child who angles her face to look to where Izzy points.

The rattle of air moving quickly through the chinks in the old outbuilding coincides with the bustle of suddenly alarmed birds in the rafters. The snap of wings above precedes the scratching of dry feet. And the taunting laughter of the bullies loses some of its power when the room darkens perceptibly, though not dramatically. A cloud may have drifted below the sun.

But when the light diminishes enough to near drown the children in shadow, the commotion of the birds beneath the cement roof ascends to a storm of frantic wings.

The face of Izzy's friend blanches in alarm and one of the other girls looks up to where Izzy indicates, where so many birds now shriek and thrash. And the girl's face hitches with concern. Enough to prevent her from speaking or warning the others.

In her mother's dream, in that dim, greyish atmosphere, Izzy is dressed in her school uniform. She walks across the vicarage lawn towards the wooded grove. Absolute silence grips the scene until, from the trees, there drifts an ethereal piping she's heard before in her sleep.

Jess is watching her daughter from behind the murky glass of the French windows, where she sits in a wheelchair wearing her client's crumpled leisure suit, the velvet worn threadbare. Her attempt to stand up is instinctive but rendered futile by the Velcro straps that restrain her wrists and ankles.

Jess tries to call out to Izzy with all her might but is mute, her open mouth no more than a silent void. Her desperation to call to her daughter only succeeds in reopening her facial scar. Warm blood runs over her chin and floods the gaps where her teeth are missing.

Out on the lawn, Flo joins Izzy and stands beside her. But this is Flo when younger. Freed from a wheelchair, her back is straight, her posture erect. The elegant Flo from the photographs in the bureau takes the little girl's hand. Izzy looks up at Flo adoringly as if at her mother. Together they then turn their heads to the great and restless trees.

Haggard, beaten and trapped inside the old vicarage, Jess tries again to call but no sound exists here save the piping.

A glimmer of a figure enters her peripheral vision. Someone dressed in a white nightgown seeps from the darkness and appears behind Jess's head and shoulders. From the sleeves of the gown, a pair of emaciated forearms extend and two veiny hands settle upon her shoulders. Flo again, but a woman with arms ghastly and aged enough to have just assisted in her rise from among the dead.

Jess looks up, and in the darkness above her there is only a gleam of dirty teeth where a face should be.

Pulled so fast that her breath is stolen from out of her broken mouth, she and the wheelchair are hauled backwards and into the unlit vicarage.

Pointing at the iron sky beyond the dirty glass of the storeroom, Izzy mouths the word 'Erce', and the light dims until only the bright edges and glimmering planes of the broken desks survive oblivion.

The confidence of the bullies drains with the light. Their tittering and chatter subside at the sudden onset of their blindness. In the dark they fidget, shuffle and bump against each other.

The dead bird between Izzy's feet flaps awake as if emerging from a paralysing shock and explodes upwards into a flurry of snap-cracking wings. As if the risen bird's panic is contagious, those in the rafters shriek in unison and careen in terror and a haste to escape their roost.

Whatever comes to settle upon the roof of the building eclipses what remains of the dimming rectangle of the skylight.

The room instantly fills with the intense swooping of the trapped, routed pigeons. Their dusty wings bat and flap around the heads of the children, their tiny bodies thump into unseen walls.

Heads down and screaming, the two boys dash from the room by leaping for a memory of where the door once was. The three girls remain behind, transfixed.

Izzy smiles at what has been instigated here and mouths 'Erce' again. The whirling birds part around her.

Somewhere in the dark, a girl screams and her face jerks as if she can't breathe through the seizure of terror that has engulfed her. Passing birds scrape her face. Her hair is raked out in the turbulence of so many frantic wings. Urine spatters her black shoes and white ankle socks.

Only now does Izzy falter into surprise, startled by what she has done when cornered and consumed by rage and fear. Quickly, her raised hand winds a circle clockwise.

The birds find an escape route. The wake of their flight fades and a profound silence falls. Every molecule of air and every wave and ripple of sound might have been sucked from the room. In the space that then brightens by near imperceptible increments, two of the girls are revealed to be sitting on the floor with their hands clutched to their ears. Inconsolable, they issue sobs unheard within the vacuum.

Izzy stands upright in the middle of the room, unaffected by anything but surprise at herself. She stares at the bone wheel in her palm.

The silence ends in the passing of a heartbeat and into the old storeroom comes the bedlam of crying, frightened girls.

As the phone trills and vibrates on the bedside table, Jess sits up in bed. Eyes wide, she heaves air into her lungs. Then slaps her hands about the bed covers, reorienting herself within her surroundings. Awareness dawns that she's inside her bedroom at home and not trapped within a wheelchair in darkness. Her eyes briefly close in relief and she unleashes a single sob before calming.

She snatches up her baying phone. The number for 'IZZY SCHOOL' is calling.

20

School gates fit for a high-security prison swing closed automatically, crashing and rattling within the frame. The shuddering gate passes a judder through the spiked fence posts thrusting outwards at the summit of the long barrier.

Outside the steel palisade, Jess lowers herself to one knee so her eyes can meet Izzy's. Or would do if her daughter didn't insist on dolefully gazing at her feet.

'What happened, Izz? What was them kids on about?'

Izzy shrugs.

'Izzy, I want you to tell me what you did. They was scared half to death. I don't understand. It don't make no sense to the teachers. What did you say to those girls? You must have said something to frighten them like that.'

Unable to look at her mother, Izzy mumbles, 'It all just come. Like a dream.'

'What did? They said you brought the bird? Put a devil in their eyes? What's that mean?'

Izzy shrugs again.

'I've asked you a question. Now answer it.'

With no way out of the interrogation, Izzy's eyes well with tears and her face crumples. It's not the response Jess wants and only when she gives Izzy's shoulder a little shake does Izzy look up, before shouting a response broken by sobs. 'They wouldn't leave me alone! You said they would if I hid! I hid! I did! They still stole from me! Pushed me over! You keep making me come back!'

'Oh, my love. My sweet love.' Jess is stricken enough by her daughter's confession to cry herself. She tries to draw Izzy into an embrace.

Izzy twists free of her hands. 'I want Daddy! I want my daddy. He'll shout at them!'

'Izz. We been through it. My love—'

'They keep hurtin' me! Every day! An' Flo helped me.'

For a moment Jess doesn't speak, is rendered speechless. When she manages to form a sentence, her voice is breathless. 'Izz? What you mean, Flo helped you? Izz? Tell me.'

'Told me to say things. To make it stop.'

'What things?'

'Words.'

Jess stands up, her face now so drawn with sleep deprivation and stress she can only gaze at Izzy as if her daughter is another mother's child.

21

*W*ith the hand that is not incessantly pulling at a strand of her fringe, Jess holds her phone. She bites her bottom lip as she waits for a call to be answered. When it is, her shoulders sag with relief. 'Oh, Pen. Love. Hiya. I'm after a big favour. Really sorry. Got problems up Izzy's school.'

'Not them bloody girls again.'

'Yeah. That's about the size of it. And I gotta work tonight again. Sheila won't bloody listen. Anyways, can you take Izz? Just for tonight and drop her up—'

'You know I would, any time. But we're out tonight. Anniversary. We ain't had a night together in ages.'

'Oh, shit. Sorry. I totally forgot.'

'It don't matter, Jess.'

'You know anyone else who can take her tonight? Just tonight?'

'I don't. Sarah would have done but she's got mine.'

Jess looks at the ceiling in exasperation, or despair, and closes her eyes as if the thump of drums against the ceiling risks damage to her sight as well as hearing.

Izzy's voice startles her back into the room. 'I want to go to Flo's.'

Jess turns and meets her daughter's eyes that are still red from crying.

'I don't want to go to Penny's!'

As the front door of Nerthus House closes behind Morag on her way out, waning sunlight pierces the stained glass of the spoked wheel fanlight.

Weary Jess plods the hallway. Still sullen from the spat that began in the flat and continued to spark on the bus journey here, Izzy drifts behind her mother. By the time they've shuffled into the living room, Jess's expression stiffens. There is evidence of the stern resolve that she will adopt in her care of Florence Gardner and her landfill of a home, in the form of the supermarket bags that bulge beneath her hands. One is filled with light bulb boxes, the other cleaning equipment.

At the threshold of the living room, Jess contrives the manner of a woman determined to be decisive. Strict, if necessary, to get through another night with the disturbed client in the wheelchair who inhabits this baffling, creepy place that makes no sense.

'Hello-lo-lo, Flo!' from Izzy, whose spirits revive and shoot vertical into elation at the sight of Flo.

Flo only turns her head at the sound of Izzy's voice and the intensity of the elderly woman's reaction disarms Jess. Abruptly alert, eyes shining, she beams at the little girl. There's no mistaking the heartfelt expression of joy lighting up the sunken face that doesn't appear to have had much to smile about in years. 'Merry meet!' she cries out. Following the greeting with 'Cup of tea, Mother' that Jess assumes is directed at her.

Izzy scampers into the room and kneels beside the wheelchair. To Jess's continuing amazement, Flo takes the little girl's hands and holds them on her lap.

Fascinated but excluded from this new bond that gives her tormented client so much pleasure, Jess turns her attention to the ceiling. She bites her bottom lip, places her bags on the floor and leaves the room.

Outside in the hall, she slips a hand on the banister and takes a step up, into the dark.

Jess silently returns to the lounge but maintains a distance from her client and daughter, to observe Izzy interacting with Flo and how each is smitten with the other. Their heads are closer together than before, and Flo appears to be inspecting one of Izzy's drawings that she has laid upon Flo's lap. Jess also catches the end of something that Izzy is sharing with the elderly woman. 'No. Not any more. He come out of prison and had to live in another flat. He's too angry. But not with me.' When Izzy senses her mother's presence, she stops talking.

Jess approaches the pair and they both appear irritated, as if she's intruding. 'Izz. Give Flo these.' Jess fans three photographs in her hands. Pictures taken from Flo's collection.

Izzy leaps up to collect them and is instantly agape at their contents. 'Who are they?'

'Think she's remembering her own little girl. She thinks you're her.'

Izzy carefully places the first photograph on Flo's lap. Jess keenly watches her client's face for a reaction. 'These might help you remember, Flo. Happier times.'

Flo's face lights up with an eagerness to see what Izzy has given her. A black-and-white picture of Flo and her two children. Here the girl is around Izzy's age. Flo doesn't speak. She touches the paper with one hand, takes Izzy's fingers with the other.

Jess draws closer to the chair. Stands on the opposite side to Izzy. 'She knows. She still knows her beautiful girl.'

Izzy places a second photograph in Flo's hand. A colour picture of the celebration. Outside the loose ring of happy women in the vicarage garden, young Flo sits beside a woman almost as old as she is now. 'Mother,' she says.

Jess peers out and through the open patio doors and to the distant grove. 'This was out there?'

'What they all doin'?' Izzy asks.

'Exalted,' Flo whispers, her face animated.

The enigmatic remarks are meaningless to Jess. And after a moment of what looks like bewilderment, Flo resumes her self-absorbed gazing at the garden, perhaps trying to recall something or even catch again what she has just recalled before it vanished.

Izzy thumps across the room to the door. 'Going to the toilet. Back in a minute, Flo!'

Flo lets the pictures drop from her hand to the floor.

Jess instinctively bends to retrieve the fallen photographs.

A flash of movement and Flo swings her whole upper body behind a swiping blow at her carer's head.

SNAP.

Hyper-alert, Jess catches the old wrist in one hand. Holds it firm in a fisted grip and whispers, 'Don't you fucking dare.'

Flo relaxes, smiles at Jess and mutters, 'Erce. Erce. Erce.' Then gently rocks back and forth. So old, so frail, so reduced.

Jess keeps hold of her client's arm. 'You can play me up all you like. Not her. Never. Or else. I ain't so far from not givin' a shit. I know you're listenin', yeah?'

At the sound of the toilet flushing upstairs, Jess releases Flo's thin wrist. 'She's all I got. She's everything to me.'

Izzy bumps down the stairs outside, her excitable voice preceding her entrance. 'Flo! Flo, guess what!'

22

*F*ace strained and hair mussed, Jess dips her hand inside the murky shade of the last light fitting on the ground floor, inside the porch. She drops the exhausted bulb, its glass a musty brown, into the bag at the foot of the collapsible steps, then slips the new bulb into the socket. She steps down and hits the switch inside the hallway.

More light banishing more shadows. The dirty, messy space of the entire reception and both sides of the threshold blazes with white light. Nothing can hide or trip her up down here again.

As she passes the old mouth of the living room, she peers inside from the doorway and catches sight of Izzy in conference with Flo. Izzy sits before the wheelchair footplates and looks up at Flo as if listening intently, though Flo's lips do not move. When Izzy resumes drawing on a sketch pad, Jess moves on, wearily shaking her head.

Proud Nerthus House at dusk.

Across the road, those who watch the vicarage's transformation see windows beaming golden. Not only has the grin at ground level broadened but the eyes are open and alight upstairs. A watcher may remark that after sleeping for so long, the building appears to have been roused from within.

As another fresh bulb clicks into place inside the bathroom, the illumination of the first-floor landing is further improved. Jess steps off the stool, her relief manifest until she catches sight of the drawing of that ghastly blind beggar with one hand, forever pulling a cart through a night-blackened wood. Towards the water. Towards the dark shape that rises from the pond.

In the corner of her eye, the rusty scythe on the wall glimmers dully. Jess turns her back on it all.

Plates and pans drip suds on a draining rack. Two rubbish sacks bulge upon the floor. The washing machine thrums, spins its drum. Outside, the sky bruises at the concussion of night.

As Jess furiously scrubs the surfaces of Morag's mess from the previous shift, she shares her thoughts with Izzy, who has wandered in. 'How does a grown woman make so much mess?'

'Morag's a lazy bitch.'

'Izzy!'

Izzy runs a tap and holds Flo's drinking bottle under the stream. 'Flo's thirsty.'

'How'd you know?'

'She told me.'

Jess stops rubbing at a cup-ring and watches her daughter. 'Since you're such good mates with Flo you can help give her a bath. She'll sleep better.'

'Okay.'

'Maybe she won't be so free with her hands either if you're there. But you be careful round her, Izz. I mean it.'

'Okay.'

23

Hunched, wasted, naked, at her most frail, Flo sits perched upon a cushioned stool beside the old bathtub in a bathroom that has never been modernised. Izzy stands beside the stool and holds Flo's hand. Jess finishes sprinkling an ancient jar of pink salts into the water and turns to collect Flo. Her movements are less wary with Izzy present and she raises the body of her client in the way that a mother would lift her child.

There are grab rails around the bath and Izzy places Flo's hands upon the rails. Flo and Izzy giggle as Flo's legs slide beneath the surface.

'Not too hot?' Jess asks.

'She's fine,' Izzy answers.

'Erce. Erce. Erce,' Flo mutters, smiling with delight and swishing her lumpy hands through the gently steaming water.

'I'll do her hair and all. About time we called a chiropodist too. Now don't you let her go for a swim while I'm fetching towels, Izz.' Jess steps out of the bathroom and up to the airing cupboard, directly outside the bathroom door. With the cupboard door open, half of Flo's body and the bathtub remain visible. Izzy sits on the stool beside the bath.

Jess locates the nightdresses and selects a fresh garment from the pile. When she raises several of the clean, thick towels from the rear of the deep linen cupboard, an unusual object at the back of the dark space catches her eye. A collection of sticks and a wooden bowl.

Jess creates a shadowy gap in the wall of towels, bed linen and nightwear, and reveals another small shrine. Similar to the installation she discovered in the dining room tunnel the night before, this wheel is woven from sticks. A grotesque and primitive arrangement that has been deliberately hidden. At the centre of the circle lies another aged linen parcel, stained by what resembles old blood.

Aghast, Jess can only stare for a while at the grotesque centrepiece, the parcel, before reaching inside the cupboard to gingerly finger the dirty linen bundle.

If Jess was to look around the open door of the closet and into the bathroom, she would see Flo's entire body gradually rise from the bath water at the very same time that she raises the parcel.

Flo maintains a cross-legged position. In mid-air.

Flo levitates above the steaming water.

Wall tiles are visible beneath her folded legs, as skinny as a calf's. Nothing supports her weight. She sits in empty air. Her wasted arms rise at her sides and she turns her palms to face the ceiling.

Only Izzy can see how much Flo has altered physically. The woman's aged face appears deranged and fearsome, yet somehow elated at the same time. And as Flo grins so horribly she reveals yellow teeth, embedded in black gums.

Izzy watches in childlike awe to the beat of the water dripping from Flo's hovering body. And, as if instructed by Flo, she also holds her little arms and hands in the same position as the elderly woman who is suspended above the old bathtub.

Wincing with distaste, Jess unwraps the parcel. Hair-clippings, a man's cuff-links and a pair of desiccated, shrivelled lumps, about the same size as human eyes or testicles, lie inside the stiff wrapper.

Disgusted, Jess drops the parcel, then shoves it back onto the twig-wheel and seals the shrine with a stack of towels. She backs away from the cupboard and slowly closes the door.

Matching the smooth speed of the closing door, Flo's levitating form descends. And, with a rippling sound, her body re-enters the water of the bath.

Distracted by her shock, Jess hasn't seen the unnatural movements of her client and pushes the cupboard door fully closed until she hears a click.

Inside the bath, Flo resembles her old self again. She turns her head to Jess on the landing. 'Out now.'

As if summoned by her master, Izzy leaps off the stool to offer assistance.

24

Wearing a fresh nightgown, the white cotton patterned with yellow flowers, and her hair newly brushed and neat, Flo sits up in her bed. Once more, she's silent and her expression is dour. Her eyes comb the darkened windows overlooking the garden.

Jess nods at Izzy who slips a red thong around Flo's wattled neck. At the end of the cord hangs a white plastic oval. 'SOS' is imprinted on the front of the necklace.

Jess checks a handset that resembles an old mobile phone. She turns the screen to Izzy, who crowds her mum. A red dot is visible on the handset's screen. 'See that red dot? That's Flo. I'll be keeping my eye on it. I could lose her in this bloody mess and never find her again. Oughta put one on you an' all.'

Jess presses a button and the device beeps, primed.

'Now, come on. Jim-jams. Bed. Bit of story.'

Hours later, Jess returns to the landing from the staircase and plods to the master bedroom, a steaming cup of black coffee gripped in one hand. She walks through the treacle of sleep deprivation. Fatigue, compounded by her exertions in restoring light to Nerthus House, as well as cleaning the vicarage bathroom and kitchen, slows her movements to leaden. She pauses outside the door of Charlotte Gardner's old bedroom and peeks in.

Izzy's fast asleep and clutching Bamboo, her panda.

Jess sways as she walks to her armchair in the corner of Flo's bedroom. Dim light from a side lamp angled down guides her unsteady passage to the chair. Her heavy eyes move to take in the ceiling, the walls, the open door. In anticipation of another night at the vicarage, she takes a deep breath.

As if it's holding its own breath in anticipation, not a sound emerges from the vast house.

A fan of bills is spread on the side table beside the estate agent's brochure of the new apartment complex. Jess tries to distract herself from her thoughts of the night ahead by making a list on a notepad: preparations for moving to a new home.

Within minutes, her head drops over her chest.

She snaps awake. Wipes her mouth. Blinks hard. Returns to her papers.

Nods again. Lurches awake. But against every effort and intention, the next time her eyes close they don't reopen. Slumped in the armchair, she sleeps. And dreams.

Sunlight splices the foliage fringing the glade and probes inside the wood. From inside the copse, when standing beside the black pond in the grove, the vicarage garden appears enchanted: a soft focus of pastel colours, misted with pollen and made radiant by a celestial light. A chorus of birds and the drone of insects add weight to the soporific atmosphere.

Soft notes from a woodwind instrument draw a naked figure out of the woods, a man, who appears at the edge of the grove. His back is ramrod straight, his flesh as pale as a cadaver. His hair is neat and shiny with brilliantine. He appears then disappears behind cover, then reappears. When he enters the glade, he stops and faces the still water of the pond.

One of his hands is missing from the wrist, the stump blackened with blood. Eyeless sockets within his handsome, even face hopelessly direct their missing gaze at the water. Tears of blood encrust his cheeks. Between his legs, a loin-cloth of dark gore hangs from where his genitals have been crudely removed.

He points his stump at the pond.

Jess wakes with a start and pants with relief at having broken from the nightmare. The first thing she sees is Flo in her bed. Sleeping. But Jess is soon frowning. *Why is it so light?* Surely it cannot be morning? She just dozed off. The night couldn't have passed so . . .

Sunlight pours around and between the drapes in a shaft of ethereal light, just as it did between the boughs of the wooded grove in her dream.

From behind her chair, a naked male body extends into the space behind Jess and leans over her shoulder. The mutilated, naked man from the dream. The eyeless head, the hair perfect and face encrusted with blood, settles next to Jess's ear and whispers. 'My missing parts.'

Jess turns and her face almost touches the horrid, bloodless flesh of the figure. Black chest hair. Ransacked crotch, bearded with crimson ruin.

He speaks again. 'Have you seen them? They took things.'

Only then does Jess scream.

Jess sits up, eyes wide, and she inhales with all of her strength as if she's choking. Clutching at her face, she peers between her spread fingers and observes the empty bed in the darkened room. The bed of the elderly client that she should have been watching.

She thrashes out of her chair, disrupting the contents of the side table, then bends to snatch up the tracking handset.

The screen indicates that Flo is thirty metres behind her. That would be outside. In the garden. *Up the garden!*

Jess turns and tears the curtains aside. A window is already open and cast wide. But through it she sees only darkness, a void. A palsy shakes her shoulders and overcomes her arms and hands. She steps back from the glass.

Bumping. Yes, there is also bumping. But coming from somewhere within the house, though not this room.

Charlotte's room.

Izzy!

In moments, Jess is standing outside the closed door of Charlotte Gardner's old room.

Another soft thump issues from the other side.

Jess throws the door wide and onto darkness. 'Izz?' She slaps on the light and peers into the veritable 1970s time capsule of a girl's bedroom, her vision immediately groping for the bed.

It is empty. The sleeping bag forms an open mouth, its contents discharged, missing.

Jess stumbles inside as her little girl's voice, the sound strained and thickened, speaks from the far side of the room. 'She's rising.'

Jess starts, then turns to the voice.

Her little girl is upended in a perfect handstand, her feet resting against the wall, her face reddening from the pressure of blood in her head while holding that position. 'We have to give to the water,' she says, upside down. Izzy then peels elegantly from the wall and stands like a trained gymnast, her hands extended from her sides. The girl's eyes have a glassy faraway look and only now does Jess comprehend what her daughter is wearing. Another girl's clothes. Little Charlotte's clothes from the '70s. They must be. They are. It's the very outfit that Flo's daughter was wearing in one of the photographs Jess found in the bureau.

'Oh, Jesus. Oh, Jesus Christ.' Jess covers her cheeks with spread fingers and staggers backwards as Izzy approaches her. Frightened of her own daughter, she retreats, stumbling to the wall, where she cowers.

Izzy glides forward, smiling, and again assumes the pose of a competent young gymnast after a routine, her arms thrown back, chest out, chin raised. She stares through her mother.

Jess manages to raise a hand and wipes it before Izzy's eyes. The girl doesn't blink. Not even the rapid beeps of the SOS handset that is tracking Flo disturb her.

Forcing composure and moving on the legs of a sleepwalker herself, Jess leads her daughter to the master bedroom. Hurriedly, Jess settles Izzy on Flo's bed then returns her attention to the handset. Flo must be right outside the house now, in the garden below.

Jess flees the room, only pausing to shut the bedroom door behind her.

Holding an unlit torch, Jess approaches the closed French windows of the living room. Only pausing to wonder how Flo got outside if the doors are locked from the inside.

She unlocks the doors. Pale, and trembling in anticipation of what she might see outside, she leaves the house. Her attempt to call out to her client hisses into a whisper. 'Flo. Flo. Love.' Jess can't make herself walk any further than the patio edge. She flicks on the torch and white light extends around her.

Her face a grimace of fearful expectation, she scans the lawn around the rear of the house and peers up the garden towards the distant grove.

Nothing. No one out here. Flo should be right here, visible and now within ten metres of her position. But there is nothing. No one.

The only movement out here is directly behind and above Jess's head, one storey up. Up there, even though the indistinct limbs of the climber blend with the night, what appendages extend from the floral nightgown allow the frail figure to move sideways, as deftly as a crab and as meticulously as a probing spider. Crouched over, the head low, the thin dark form scrambles across the narrow roof that cowls a bay window, before crawling up a wall. The patchy hair is as pale as the widened eyes. Teeth are bared within the face that peers down at its carer for just a moment before the figure soundlessly slips inside the master bedroom.

Upon the mighty trees at the end of the garden, the furthest extent of Jess's torchlight plays but is too feeble to reveal much of anything. And yet the intrusion of electric light provokes something from inside the trees. Jess can clearly hear the sound of distant water swishing about a large form, either rising or sinking.

She retreats inside the vicarage. Closes the patio doors, douses her torch and withdraws from the glass, her breathing so hard she's near asthmatic with fear.

As if any sound will make her shatter, she tiptoes through the vicarage, up the stairs, across the landing and slips inside the master bedroom.

Where Flo sleeps peacefully. Impossibly, her client is here. A glance at the handset becomes an appalled scrutiny that reveals the red dot, signifying Flo, has indeed returned to the bedroom.

On top of the covers and still dressed in Charlotte Gardner's clothes from the 1970s, Izzy is nestled into Flo's back, smiling within her own deep sleep.

Unable to blink, Jess stares aghast at her client and daughter. She slips her fingers over her scarred mouth to stifle her sobs.

Curiosity overriding shock, she gathers herself sufficiently to creep to the open window and to look down at the drop to the patio below. She closes her eyes and the window.

25

*T*he rain-speckled bus window overlooks the grey smear that is the world. Sat in the window seat, Izzy's eyes flick across a landscape that increasingly urbanises and darkens, casting its shadows and symbols and abrupt noises at her glum face. With her shoulder she holds her sleep-deprived mother upright. Mum's dozed off, her long face weary from defeat. A faint whistling passes through Jess's nose.

A flicker of white on waste ground outside, between two buildings, catches Izzy's eye and makes her alert. When the next space between two soot-shaded facades appears, Izzy eagerly peers into the gully and the waste ground beyond. When the wheezing bus slows in traffic, for just a moment, she glimpses a distant figure dressed in white. Izzy smiles.

The figure acquires more detail the harder she looks. Impossibly, Flo is there and dressed in her gown from the night before. Upright with her arms raised from her sides and her palms uppermost, her feet hover a short distance from the soil and patchy weeds.

Izzy's eager fidgeting to see more of the figure wakes Jess, who comes round, blinking. She looks at Izzy then follows her daughter's eyes.

When Jess sees Flo in the distance, framed between the two buildings, the elderly woman's spindly arms are drawing circles in the air. The aged face has tilted back and her mouth either gulps at the sky or cries for help.

Bewildered by the apparition, Jess stands up. She tugs open the top window. From the distance, a piped and bony melody pierces the open slot in which drizzle and cold air spray.

'You mind?' a gruff voice announces from behind her seat.

The bus lurches, tipping Jess forward then planting her back in her seat. The figure of Flo vanishes from sight as the bus ambles on. Behind Jess, the irritated passenger stands up and slams shut the little window.

Jess turns to her daughter and for a few moments she can't speak. She swallows to regain some control of her voice. 'Did you see. . .'

But Izzy has lowered her face and is now engrossed in inspecting the little unicorn that dangles from the strap of her rucksack.

26

For once, she's wearing something other than the green uniform she throws on for work. Smart trousers and a blouse. Jess may also have found time to wash and style her hair but her tiredness can only be part-masked by make-up. The transformation, nonetheless, she hopes will bring her closer to becoming the legal tenant of this empty living room, with its smart laminate floorboards and pristine magnolia walls and ceilings.

She softly approaches the white curtains that drift over the balcony doors. Outside are a myriad trees, an expanse of lush grass, a brightly coloured playground. The new development is set far from a main road. No dogs are barking themselves hoarse and mad. No scooters perpetually chainsaw the air, and the ceiling isn't vibrating with a neighbour's thumping beats or feckless feet. Jess discreetly dabs a tear from the corner of an eye.

Izzy rushes into the room excitedly, her shoes booming. 'I want the front room, Mummy!'

A female estate agent, who stands in silence, out of the way against a wall, smiles at the little girl's elation. 'I think we have a winner, Mum.'

Jess kneels down and accepts her daughter's eager embrace. And as she strokes the fringe out of Izzy's animated eyes, she is both surprised and elated by this impulsive demonstration of love from her daughter. She's missed the attention. 'There's enough room in there for all your toys?'

'They'll go in here too.'

The agent laughs. Jess laughs. Izzy laughs but isn't sure what's so funny.

'There's a nice school down the road too. What you think?'

'Can we live here now?'

'No, love. Soon. Let's hope.'

'Daddy coming too?'

'Not here, love.'

The estate agent becomes uncomfortable and stiffens until she attempts to banish the awkward moment with, 'Refs are fine. I'm satisfied. Just the deposit and one month in advance.'

Jess looks up, her smile dying, though not all of her hope. 'They said end of the month would be fine for the money? Just started a new job.'

'You have priority but we can only hold it four weeks.'

Jess stands up, still gripping her daughter's hand.

'Can we go in the play-park?'

'We got a bus to catch.'

'Will we have a car when we move?'

'She wants it all!' the agent cries as she pushes herself off the wall and heads for the front door.

27

*D*espite the efforts she made with her appearance for the viewing, Jess is dead on her feet as she roots through reduced items on a supermarket shelf. Nearby, sitting on the floor of the aisle, Izzy is engrossed with a soft toy. A cat with a label attached to its ear. 'Mummy, it's Doctor Fizzle! Her birthday is the same as mine!' Beside Izzy, a promotional display bulges with the same animals, their huge eyes peering out and seeking children whose parents shop in the store. The same characters from Izzy's trading cards.

Jess's phone rings. She checks it. Tony.

She kills the ringtone and tries to hide how visibly stricken she is by the very idea of her ex.

At the end of the aisle and between the obstructions of tills, shoppers, promotional placards, a man stands on the other side of the store windows. Pale of face, tense, a raincoat hood concealing his hair, he stares at Jess, his phone still held to his ear. Tony. Jess and Izzy don't see him.

Jess throws a final item into her wire basket. 'Come on, Izz, or there'll be no time for tea and your bath.'

Sheepishly, cheekily, Izzy looks at her mother. 'Can we take this little one home?'

'No, love. We're not shopping for toys today. I'll remember him for your birthday.'

Izzy only holds the toy cat tighter.

'Come on, put it back. We need to go.'

Sulking, she turns her back on Jess, still clutching the toy.
'Izzy. Enough!'

Izzy doesn't budge.

Jess takes a breath and peers about herself, uncomfortable with attracting attention. 'Your mum's gotta save every penny if we're gonna live in that nice flat.'

Still no response from Izzy, who won't release the cat toy. 'Izzy? What's got into you? Put it back.'

Refusing to meet her mother's eye, Izzy continues to pet the beaming, bug-eyed cat.

Jess snaps, swoops down, yanks the cat from Izzy and tosses the toy at the display stand. The toy misses, bounces off a shelf and hits the floor.

Izzy's face reddens and crumples. From a sniffle she's soon crying hard.

Jess closes her tired eyes. Opens them only to stare at, or through, the floor. Having now gone through her overdraft of patience, sympathy and compassion, she wrestles with anger and is aquiver as she strains to hold herself together. When she looks again upon her sobbing daughter, her eyes drift to Izzy's old school shoes, relentlessly polished and mended at home. Eyes creasing and on the verge of tears, she gently touches her forehead as if in pain.

As if she's mad or cruel, a passing shopper, an elderly woman, peers at her and the judgemental scrutiny forces Jess to conceal her distress, before striding towards the till. Still crying, Izzy rises from the floor and races after her mum.

Tony has vanished from the other side of the window.

Jess strides away from the supermarket. Izzy scampers after her mother, still sniffling. 'Mummy, Mummy. You're just leaving me!'

'Not in the mood, Izz.'

'Daddy!'

Instantly alert, Jess spins about, her expression transformed from stifled anger to caution, and sees Tony lower himself to one knee and scoop up his daughter. 'Christ.'

Izzy wraps herself around her father, laughing. Over her shoulder, Tony looks at Jess and smiles.

'What you doing here, Dad?' Muffled, from Izzy.

'Just passing through and I seen this little girl bouncing away and I thought, I know them pigtails. That's my kitten. And who is this? Stowaway. Jumped in me pocket as I tried to leave the shop.' Tony offers up the Doctor Fizzle soft toy that Izzy has just been coveting. Izzy shrieks with delight. Tony rises to his feet, holding Izzy's hand, still smiling and mock-bemused by the coincidence of happening across his ex and daughter in the street. 'Where you been, kiddo?'

'We went to look at—'

'Izzy!'

Izzy stops talking and guiltily peers at her mother.

Jess refuses to look at Tony and becomes nervy, her voice losing its edge. 'It's not a Daddy day, Izz. Say hello but we gotta get on.'

Izzy looks up at Tony to see what he thinks about that. 'Soon, Daddy, when you're not angry any more, I'll be coming to see you every weekend.'

Tony's expression hitches on a rictus more than a smile. He glares at Jess. 'Not soon enough for me, Kid. I miss you so much it hurts your old dad right here.' Tony taps his heart then leans over and kisses Izzy on top of her head. Izzy hugs her father's waist.

Jess turns away, her jaw clenched as the conversation continues behind her back.

'Every day I don't see you, bit of me heart chips off an' all.'

'Where does it go?' Izzy asks.

Through gritted teeth Jess lowers her voice but almost wants it to carry. 'Comes out with the rest of the shit he talks.' She swivels about and stares intently into her daughter's eyes. 'Izz. Now.' Izzy breaks from her father's embrace and returns to Jess, though is mostly entranced by the new toy. 'You can speak to your dad another time. I've already explained this.'

Her awareness of her mother's distress dawns and she falls sheepish as Jess begins to haul her away. But Izzy also can't resist a look back, over her shoulder at her dad, who continues to shuffle up the pavement in their wake.

'Even though I ain't always there, Izz, what I never forget is how much I love you and your mum. You're the little girl we brought into this world together.'

Jess snaps her head to the side but still won't look at Tony. 'Tone. Please.'

'And you, kitten, are everything to me. So we all gotta work through this bad time, yeah?'

'Yeah!'

'Me and your mum have to. For you.'

Jess stops her retreat along the high street. Bends down to Izzy, who looks shocked at the expression on her mother's face. 'Stay here. Right here. Don't move.'

'Why?'

'Cus I bloody says so. I need to say something to your dad.'

Warily, Jess shuffles to Tony and finally meets his eyes. By the time she's suppressed her fear sufficiently to speak, her voice is no more than a whisper. 'Tone, please. You can't tell her things like that. Building up her hopes.'

'She needs her dad. You and me can work the rest of it out. Like I told you before.'

Jess closes her eyes in a failed attempt to temper her despair. But Tony isn't discouraged. 'Longer we're apart, more she suffers. We both need to think of what's best for her.'

Tony's eyes ferret into the shopping bag in Jess's hand and when he spots the red LAST DAY sticker on a loaf of bread, the sight seems to break his heart. He fishes out his wallet. Thumbs out a fifty-pound note. 'Here. Been a good week.'

Jess recoils. 'We're all right.'

'Take it. Extra. On top of what's gonna be transferred this month. Let me help. Please.'

Jess reluctantly and carefully takes the money without touching Tony's fingers before turning and hurrying back to Izzy, who is doing more than observing another tense exchange between her parents; she's concentrating hard enough to be studying them. Jess snatches Izzy's hand.

Tony pads behind his ex and daughter. 'I can come round later. Bring Chinese.'

'Mummy! Yes! Yes!'

Jess doesn't look back. 'No, ta. We gotta get early nights. Both of us.'

Izzy looks at her father one last time, her little face stiffening with concern and sympathy for her thwarted father. But her dad isn't looking at her any more; he's staring at the back of her mum's head instead, as if he is calling upon every last reserve to quell his temper. Only when he notices Izzy's scrutiny does his expression transform into a reassuring smile. He winks.

28

Upon the kitchen counter, Jess's phone trills and grinds out vibrations. Again. Jess picks it up, only to mute the handset before deactivating it and tossing it aside. She turns off the overhead lights, pads to the window and gently parts the blinds at one side.

In the street outside the block, Tony's car is parked at the kerb. Through the railings and through the windscreen, he's just visible with one arm raised, holding a phone against his ear. Jess drops the blinds and swivels to rest her back against the nearest wall. In the darkened kitchen she slides down the wall until she's sitting, gripping ankles pulled tight against the back of her thighs. She wipes at the trickles glimmering on her cheeks. As a long sigh escapes between her disfigured lips, she checks her watch and struggles to her feet and heads out of the kitchen.

In her daughter's bedroom down the hall, Jess finds Izzy standing by the bed, only half dressed and preoccupied with the new toy. Neatly folded pyjamas lie undisturbed on the duvet.

The sight of Izzy coveting the gift from Tony blanches Jess with an anger she barely manages to suppress. 'You ain't done your teeth. Nothing. You ain't ready for bed like I asked you.'

'I am!'

'Don't look like it. Where's your jams?'

'I will.'

'Will what? You ain't even listening. Put that down and get changed. Come on. Now. Ain't tellin' you again.' Jess bends over and starts picking discarded clothes off the floor. 'I need to say something. About your dad. He knows he's not supposed to be here, or up your school. You know that.'

'Cus he's angry. Not with me.'

The last statement slips out quietly enough to pass for sly and Jess bristles. 'Never mind back-chat. You just say hello if you see him, but you don't go anywhere with him. Never. Nowhere. You hear?'

Izzy doesn't turn her head or react. Still reluctant to get ready for bed, she leaves the room and heads for the bathroom.

To the sounds of a tap running and the buzzing of an electric toothbrush, Jess is left alone to mull over whether she's been heard or she needs to press her instructions further. She opts for a reinforcement of her message from the door of her daughter's bedroom. 'You stay in school. You only leave with Penny. Or me. No one else. Your dad's having problems. He has to stay away from us for a bit till he's sorted himself out. Yeah? We've been through it before, Izz. I know you understand.'

Izzy doesn't reply.

Jess sighs and stares at the spectacle of herself in her daughter's oval wall-mirror. After two sleepless nights and the endless frustrations of her days with Flo, what she sees startles her. She swipes her hair back, sits on the bed and rubs at her scar. Then clenches and unclenches her hands until the toilet flushes. Jess stares at the back of her red hands. They look so old. Too old for a woman of her age.

Izzy comes in, leaps onto the bed and winds behind Jess as she moves up to the pillow.

'Can I ask you something, Izz? About last night? Mmm?'

'Yeah.'

'What does Flo say to you? What you two always whispering about?'

'Just things.'

'What things?'

'About the garden. House. It don't make much sense.'

'You remember anything from last night? Mmm? The sleepwalking?'

Izzy shakes her head but is fascinated with herself. 'What did I do?'

'Never mind.'

'I want to know!'

'You was walking about. Nothing else. But did you know Flo was outside? So how did she get outside?'

'She walked?'

'You seen her walk?'

Jess can't see the mischievous smile on her daughter's face, until she turns her upper body to interrogate the sudden silence behind her head. 'Have you seen her walk?'

'No. But I seen her float.'

'I'm being serious, Izz. What else does Flo say to you?'

'She calls me Charlotte.'

Jess nods and tries to suppress her alarm. 'Half hour with the pad. Then off to sleep.'

Izzy's face cracks into a big smile. 'Can I come with you to Flo's tomorrow?'

'No chance. School. You're lucky they had you back. Penny's picking you up too. Penny, not your dad, yeah?'

'Can I come see Flo after school?'

Jess closes her eyes with frustration. 'Jams on. Now. Final request or the pad's leaving with me.'

Not long after Jess has managed to fall asleep in her bedroom, the space barely lit by the ambient glow in the hall, her lips move and mutter at the onset of a dream. A dream heralded by the bony piping of a single distant note. A dream in which two figures walk between the trees surrounding the grove, towards the still, black water of the pond. A man and a child.

It's the strange bloodless man again, naked, his flesh so white. His eyes remain holes caked in dried blood and his groin is still a black, misshapen wound. He stands with an aristocratic bearing, and his empty sockets defiantly confront Jess, the watcher. Izzy stands beside him, smiling. She is once again dressed as Charlotte Gardner and she holds the bloodied stump of the man's arm that is missing a hand.

'It's time,' the man says, and Izzy and her grisly companion approach the pond.

Jess again finds herself secured within Flo's wheelchair, her ankles and wrists restrained by straps. But this time, the chair is half-submerged in the pond. From what she can see of her own chest and arms and hands she is dressed in Flo's ratty leisure suit and her body has aged horribly, is now elderly, her arms as thin as flutes, her skin near transparent. 'No. Oh, Christ, no!' she calls out, but though her face is screaming, her words are the faint, faltering entreaties of an old woman. They reverse and slide down her throat.

Izzy and the blind, mutilated man wade into the shallows to join her.

Slowly, Jess and the wheelchair are drawn back and into deeper water. As she writhes and struggles against her bonds, the cold water rises up her body to her neck, then her chin. Before going under, she throws her head back to take a final gasp.

Jess sits up in bed, her head thrown back to complete the desperate inhalation that started in the dream in which she was being drowned. Hair sodden with sweat, she doubles over and pants for air until she catches sight of the figure beside the bed, silhouetted by faint ambient light. A form dressed in a pale gown, the small head tatty.

Flo.

Jess screams.

From out of the darkness, Izzy cries out a startled, terrified response.

Jess yanks on the bedside light. Where the ghastly silhouette of Flo was just standing she sees her daughter, hair mussed. Izzy holds the new soft toy beside her face, and when exposed to a full revelation of her terrified mother, the intensity of her wails increase until Jess is deafened.

'Baby. Baby girl. Baby.' Jess opens her arms and Izzy vaults into them and they squeeze each other as Jess sobs with relief. 'Bad dream. Mums have them too. All it was. I'm so sorry I frightened you. My love, don't you cry.'

Izzy whimpers and sniffs, her face hidden.

'All right now. Shush. Shush. Mummy's here.' Jess lies back and stares at the ceiling, coming down from shock and clutching her daughter to her chest as if she'll die before letting this child go again.

29

'Jess. A word, if you please.'

It's only when Jess hears Sheila's voice that she notices the car parked outside the vicarage. Tired after another broken night, and listless enough to need to concentrate on where she places her feet, she swings about, seeking the origin of the disembodied voice.

Her boss is alighting from her car, an eyebrow already raised. 'Your daughter not with you today?'

'Sorry. Had no choice. Short notice. It—'

'I'm not here to discuss your childcare arrangements. I'm here because of your attitude towards your client.' With an expression equalling the severity of her black suit, Sheila wastes no time in crowding Jess at the end of the front path. 'All I ever ask of my employees is that they're punctual, that they follow their brief in a professional manner. Am I asking too much, I wonder?'

'I'm just trying to make things better for Flo. Stuff needs sorting out here, Sheila.'

'My point exactly, Jess.'

'There's no assistive tech. Place is a shambles. It ain't been de-cluttered. It's too dark for her. It's—'

'When Mrs Gardner was able, she left strict instructions about her care. She wanted everything left—'

'She's living off lemon puffs. She ain't getting the right nutrition. I'm no doctor—'

'Quite!'

Chastened, Jess lowers her eyes and softens her tone. 'But I know when a client is knocked off, Sheila. She's either confused or flat. She's got delirium. Half the time the poor love must be terrified. She should be on oxygen. The notes ain't up to date. She's wandering. Hospital. It's that time.'

'You bit my hand off when I told you about the salary for this position but perhaps I need to rethink the posting.'

Jess's posture softens further and her placatory tone closes on wheedling. 'No. I really need . . . I can do it, Sheila. I just think, for Flo's sake, the appointee needs to make improvements.'

'That's not your concern.'

'It's just . . . Sheila. This place. It's, I don't know. It's not right. It's unhealthy. All wrong. And Flo. She ain't as incapacitated as it says in the notes. They're wrong. She's been wandering. Day and night. She—'

'Impossible. So is it you or your client that's suffering delusions? And by the look of your eyes, it's clear to me that it's time you took better care of yourself. Never mind your client. And you'll need to because I'm going to need a greater show of flexibility and commitment from you. Starting with you working the night shift from next week.'

'God, no.'

'What?'

'I promised Izzy. Nights is too hard on her—'

'Your personal circumstances cannot be allowed to affect your ability to perform your job. This is an important position.' And once she's paused to let that sink into her employee, while fighting the flicker of a smile that might even be an expression of satisfaction, Sheila returns to her car and stuffs herself inside it. She hasn't finished with Jess, though, and peers out of the driver's side window to issue a final reprimand. 'And, for the love of God, don't touch Morag's bloody chicken again!'

Mute and stupefied, Jess watches Sheila start her car. Across the road, she catches the eye of the elderly grandmother in the large sun hat. A woman she's seen out front several times. A neighbour who immediately dips her head to conceal her face beneath the brim of her hat.

Sheila pulls away but Jess remains at the kerb and continues to consider the neighbour, before crossing the lane to the hedge hemming an impressive cottage and another immaculate and vividly coloured garden.

The elderly neighbour continues to trim a long supple length of hawthorn. Around her feet, a range of gardening implements and a growing collection of sticks, cut to various lengths, are neatly laid upon a green plastic sheet. For fear that the stooped figure is unaware of her, Jess clears her throat.

A prompt for the gardener, who startles Jess by speaking without looking up. 'Nerthus House remains under a shadow. Even on a day as beautiful as this, you can see it.' The gardener straightens her back, effortlessly, without a groan or sigh. And though her eyes remain shaded by the brim of the hat, her brilliant white teeth are set in either a grimace or a grin. It's hard to tell.

She's around a decade younger than Flo and elegantly attired. Even her gardening gloves appear tailored. A fairy-tale grandmother and a tad hyper-real, as if she's a model on a brochure selling happiness, health and retirement plans. 'How is dear Florence these days?'

Jess feigns a polite smile. 'Feisty. A devil. An angel sometimes. Never predictable.'

To which the woman issues a peal of polished laughter. 'She hasn't changed then! So imperious. Mercurial Florence. I doubt even dementia could dent that.'

'You lived here long?'

'Most of my life.'

Which prompts Jess to peer around herself at the enchanting street. 'You're lucky. It's beautiful.'

'Blessed. Literally.'

As if directed there by the comment, Jess peers at the distant church spire, the neighbour following her eyes.

'Oh, the village was considered sacred long before they showed up. A Roman general once wrote of Eadric. All wooded then, reaching in every direction for miles. He claimed it was holy to the ancient Britons. Probably for millennia before other faiths washed ashore.'

'Flo has some old things. In her cabinet. Broken pots and stuff.'

'Flo's children found so much. In the waters of the grove.'

'Top of the garden?'

'Once a temple, you know. To a deity. Where offerings were made. For wisdom. Protection. Fertility. Courage.' The woman turns her face to the vicarage and her smile fades, her expression growing grave. Between her gloved fingers she twists a stick. 'You know what happened here?'

'Afraid I don't know much history.'

'With Flo?'

'Not really. Her daughter . . . Flo thinks my nipper is her daughter.'

'Little Lottie. Beautiful child. A terrible business. Florence never survived the loss of little Lottie. She merely functioned. Though we did what we could. As neighbours. Friends. Sisters, if you like.' The woman bends to take up another stick and with her nimble hands begins to trim it of leaves and buds.

'Terrible. I can't imagine . . . I don't let myself.'

The woman nods agreement. 'You know, when Florence first became ill, she told me she considered dementia a blessing. So that she could forget. Her pain. It was the last thing she said to me.' The woman sighs and casually returns to her work.

Though eager for more, Jess considers herself dismissed. She checks her watch and drifts back to the vicarage.

30

*F*lo in her chair, gazing out at the garden. No change there. But much of the glass and wood in the living room now shines from Jess's deep clean.

Working near Flo on tasks she conducts with a little anger, Jess sprays and dusts the glass-fronted cabinet that hoards the ancient shards of pottery and the weathered artefacts. The final cabinet to be cleaned. Behind her shoulder, Flo watches intently, silently, before drawing an anticlockwise circle in the air before her chair.

As Jess wipes the glass clear, the withered black hand upon the shelf passes from murk to clarity, from shadow to light, and glimmers like old leather. Newly appalled by what might not be a glove after all, Jess turns away.

From the window of Flo's bedroom, Jess peers out at the garden to check on her client.

Flo sits motionlessly on the lawn. An installation of a frail, barely living woman inside a wheelchair. She wears a red robe over a white nightdress. Her lumpy feet are concealed inside a pair of red slippers.

As ever, Flo gazes at the grove at the top of the garden. The shimmer of the pond's black water is partially visible through the fringe of trees.

'This can't go on,' Jess says and turns from the window.

She goes to the bureau, the antique article of furniture in which she found Flo's family photographs, and pulls open the drawer below the one that contained the pictures. With a clunk, it slides out as far as it can go.

Jess raises a thick folder of paper correspondence from the drawer and leafs through the bundle of letter-headed documents inside. At a glance, they're official records and statements. An administrative history.

She takes a seat on Flo's bed with the sheaf of papers and browses until she finds a wallet containing a marriage certificate for FLORENCE HARRIET GARDNER and ALGERNON WILFRED GARDNER.

Jess sets the paper aside and retrieves two more official-looking documents. Birth certificates. Two of them. One each for CHARLOTTE ISADORA GARDNER and PHILLIP ARTHUR GARDNER.

Jess takes a moment to peer at a picture of Flo with her two children, taken in the garden decades before. 'Charlotte and Phillip.'

Beneath the birth certificates lies a death certificate. Jess pulls it free and reads the scant details of Algernon Gardner's demise. A civil registry document accompanies the certificate and declares the man dead after being missing for seven years. Dated 1980.

Other documents in the same wallet reveal Flo to be the recipient of an RAF pension. Inside another slim leather wallet, Jess ferrets out an old RAF warrant card and a passport-sized picture of a man in uniform.

The sight of him forces her to gasp and she cannot prevent a slight palsy in her fingers as she raises the picture and brings it closer to her eyes. Her scrutiny confirms that this is the mutilated man who has appeared in her dreams. Flo's husband. In the picture he's dressed in an RAF uniform but there can be no mistake: this is the man she sees when she sleeps.

Jess slips the wallet back inside the folder, lurches across to the bureau and stuffs the folder back inside the drawer as if it's toxic.

She steps away. Bites her bottom lip until the flesh whitens. Then returns and extracts another elegant folder from the open drawer. This one is made from card and secured by a red ribbon. Jess retakes her seat on the bed and unties the bow.

Outside, an absolute silence thickens about Flo and her wheelchair upon the lawn. And, as if wary of being observed from on high, she turns her head to face the vicarage.

Her eyes fix upon the bedroom window.

From inside the card folder, Jess removes a second death certificate. The words swim and she has to read them three times to make sense of what she is looking at. CHARLOTTE GARDNER, aged 12, died in 1973. The cause of death is listed as ACCIDENTAL. 'Oh, Flo. You poor love.'

Jess peers at the photographs on the bureau and finds one in which Charlotte was no older than Izzy. Again, the little girl is holding her mother's hand in the garden. They appear inseparable. They always do, in any picture in which they are together. Their bond evident and poignant enough to compel Jess to wipe at an eye to wick away a tear. Her sadness only deepens when she returns her attention to the contents of the folder and disturbs the other artefacts. A child's hand-drawn picture. Birthday cards sent from the little girl to her mother. A comfort muslin. Her milk teeth in an envelope.

Jess closes the folder, reties the ribbon and folds it away. Eager to finish her investigation of her client's personal history, she flicks through a third folder stuffed with bank statements and investment documents, until she pauses and raises a letter. 'Got it.'

A COURT OF PROTECTION document. The name of the DEPUTY with LASTING POWER OF ATTORNEY for Flo is highlighted: PHILLIP ARTHUR. Flo's son's address is also cited. He lives in France. 'Your little boy.' Jess looks up at a framed black-and-white picture of young Phillip on the bureau. Solemn and awkward, always. His eyes, troubled.

Jess ferrets out her phone and adds the phone number from the document. She saves the contact: FLO'S SON. Then rummages out a bale of handwritten envelopes. She takes off the rubber band and looks through them. All are addressed to PHILLIP GARDNER at various addresses, spanning decades. All have been RETURNED TO SENDER. NO LONGER AT THIS ADDRESS.

Jess looks at the glowing windows, as if seeking a light to banish the darkness that has crept inside her from Flo's history. She closes the bureau drawer and leaves the room.

Glancing at the sunny garden through the open French windows, Jess checks on Flo and sees her client sitting in silence and gazing intently at the distant grove. Satisfied that Flo is safe, Jess peels away and pads to the front of the vicarage. She checks her SOS tracking handset to make certain that Flo hasn't moved, then pulls the front door closed, with the catch left on.

There is a distant snick of secateurs from across the road, where the top of the elderly neighbour's sun hat remains visible. Jess takes a deep breath and ambles over the lane to the opposing hedgerow. 'Sorry. Me again.'

The gardener stretches upright without a groan.

'Flo had a son too,' Jess says, then bites her lip.

As if recalling something unpleasant, the neighbour's expression stiffens. She stares until Jess feels uncomfortable enough to lower her eyes. And then the neighbour speaks. 'You spend so much time with her. More than anyone else.

You're all Flo has left now. I suppose it's only fair you know.' The elderly woman slips her pruning shears inside a pocket, then nods at Nerthus House. 'Phillip. He was at boarding school when his dear sister was lost. He joined the air force later, after school. Followed in the footsteps of his dashing father. But he never came home. Not once to my knowledge. Flew away, just like Algy.'

'Flo's husband. He passed away?'

'Not precisely. He left them and couldn't be traced. Flo had no choice but to declare him dead.' The gardener sighs. 'Devilishly handsome man. I think we all fell for him when they first moved here. But what do we know of anyone? A charmer, Algy. But cruel. A controlling man. Hateful to dear Flo. And a brute to his daughter.'

'That's awful.'

'Oh, Flo kept up appearances as he tormented her and the little girl he despised. Ever the dutiful wife. But it all came out later.'

'How did she die . . . Charlotte?'

'Swallowed a great deal of her mother's medication. Ate them like sweets. And she didn't die easily. Was ghastly. I'll never forget that day.'

'Suicide.'

'Accident, they claimed. Inconceivable then that a young girl from such a good family would take her own life.'

'Jesus.'

'It was all too late by the time Flo found her. And Flo had a concussion at the time.'

The two women exchange glances in silence until the gardener stoops over to raise a hawthorn branch. She takes her little shears from her pocket, the steel glinting, surgical in its brightness as she severs the end of the stick. The snap echoes through the silent, beautiful village.

Jess nods and offers the neighbour a pained smile. 'I better get on. But thank you. All makes a lot more sense now.' Jess pads away, humbled as she goes.

The neighbour watches her return to the vicarage. 'No matter how difficult she is to manage . . . even if she forgets herself and what she's doing . . . the past is always with her.'

31

*J*ess stiffens when the call is answered. She stops chewing her bottom lip. 'Phillip? Is that Phillip Gardner?'

'Who is calling, please?'

'I'm sorry to bother you, sir. My name's Jess McMachen. Your mum's new carer.'

A silence ensues that she tries to end.

'I just started—'

'Who told you to contact me?'

Jess paces the kitchen. 'I know I'm not supposed to call. But your mum needs better support. She's depressed, Mr Gardner. Having delusions. I think it's PTSD. You need another GP to make an assessment.'

'Please don't ever contact me again.'

'Hang on. Please. Mr Gardner, she's an old lady. I can't stand by and let this carry on.'

'Then you should leave.'

'I know people have differences—'

'You haven't the first clue about her. This is none of your business.'

'Mr Gardner, I didn't want to upset you. I'm just very worried about your mum.'

Phillip sucks in his breath. It's audible on the line. When he finally speaks his voice falters. 'She was hardly what you could call a mother after my sister died.'

The motion-detecting handset, synchronised to Flo's necklace, beeps in alarm.

'What came to her. What she became. You simply have no idea.'

From the rear, from the garden, a din of distant bird cries rises and penetrates the vicarage. 'I'm sorry, Mr Gardner. I don't follow.' Jess ferrets the device out of her pocket and winces as she confirms that Flo is on the move.

Had anyone been observing Flo in the garden, that small figure dressed in a red robe, there could be no mistake that the elderly woman just stood up before her wheelchair, in one smooth and soundless manoeuvre.

Inside the kitchen, the bird cries grow to the sound of a flock in panic. Jess makes her way to the door, her phone pressed to her ear so she can still hear Phillip Gardner's voice as it blurts through the cacophony. 'She's not to be trusted. And if you're half as observant as you appear, then you'll know about the grove.'

Within the cacophony of enraged birds, Flo turns slowly upon the lawn. Her arms are stretched out from her sides, her palms uppermost. She completes a circle. Her red robe sways.

With her head tilted back, her mouth agape and her eyes rolled up white, she begins a second circle. At its conclusion, her slippered feet leave the ground. And soon, a metre of thin air separates her toes and the grass.

She keeps rising.

Phone clamped to her ear, Jess steps through the bags of the hall, her frantic eyes peering through the living room door, across the lounge, through the French windows and into the garden where Flo's wheelchair sits empty on the lawn. 'She's wandering. Hang on.'

'You mustn't, mustn't tell her where I am.'

'She's just—' Jess dips her head. Her eyes implore the garden to reveal her client.

'All of them. Around her. They changed her. My father was never found. They got rid of him. Please don't call me again.'

As Jess's concern for her client turns to panic, Phillip ends the call. She pockets her phone and races through the living room towards the patio. A few steps from the open French windows, she catches sight of two thin legs jutting beneath the hem of Flo's red dressing gown, in the upper part of the doorframe. They hang in empty air outside, above the lawn. Distant trees in the glade are clearly visible below the slippered feet.

Jess pulls up. 'Christ!'

The body of Flo abruptly drops from the air and crumples upon the lawn, the red gown pooling.

Jess snaps from a shocked, gaping stupor. Races across the remaining few feet of the living room floor and leaps through the open French windows, into the light of the garden. Where her client lies inert upon the lawn, her limbs profoundly motionless. Flo's eyes are closed. Around the garden, birds shriek their alarm from on high.

Jess casts a nervous glance into the air in an attempt to see what it was that Flo had climbed up, or been raised by. But there is nothing there. Mystified, she drops to her knees beside her client, reaches for her hand and holds it. 'Flo. Flo. Don't move. I'll call an ambulance.' Jess fumbles her phone out of her pocket.

Within her inert head that lies upon the grass, Flo's eyes open. And before Jess is able to raise the phone, the old woman darts forward from the waist, as quick as a snake, to seize Jess's wrist and hold it fast between her jaws.

'Shit!' Jess drops the phone and tries to pull her arm free. But Flo doesn't relent and, as Jess's arm moves, Flo's scrawny body bumps across the grass, attached to her carer by the mouth.

Jess rises to a crouch and pulls more forcefully. 'Let go!'

Saliva foaming about her thin lips, her jaws locked, Flo's entire body continues to follow along the ground as Jess stumbles in retreat. She might have been dragging the weight of a small crocodile, clamped to her limb. The old mouth fastened to her wrist begins to gnaw and the biter's eyes enliven with a bestial ferocity. Jess withers from pain, from shock. Whimpers. In a last resort she draws her free hand back to strike her client.

Yet pauses. Some innate, internal reservation breaks the circuit, ends the compulsion, and she restrains herself from slapping the head of the elderly woman in her care. Instead, she slips her free hand into Flo's armpit and raises the woman's entire body from the ground. Then staggers and fumbles her onto the wheelchair. With a pained cry, she twists her arm free of Flo's moist jaws.

Beside the wheelchair, Jess sways. She can do little but stare aghast at the wet, bruised flesh of her wrist.

Flo smiles at her. Impossibly, the woman appears unhurt from the fall.

Snapping from her shock, Jess tugs the Velcro restraints around her client's emaciated ankles and wrists, on both sides. And only when her client is secured to the wheelchair does she turn her attention again to the continuing cries of the birds, so many birds. She scans the tree-line at the summit of the garden but can make no sense of the phenomenon, nor of anything else.

She grasps the handles of the chair and aims the wheelchair for the open French windows. But stops pushing when her phone trills loudly. She claws the handset from her pocket. PENNY is lit up on the screen.

32

*P*enny rolls a pushchair through the school gates with two foundation children walking beside her, each enraptured by their ice-lollies. Izzy drifts at the back of the group, staring at the bone artefact that Flo gave her while her lolly melts over her other hand.

'Hey, kitten!'

Startled by the sound of Tony's voice, both Penny and Izzy turn about.

Her father is more subdued than Izzy is used to seeing him, and paler too. One of his hands is also bandaged across the knuckles. Yet Izzy is elated to see him. She pockets the carving and leaps towards her father.

Penny struggles to share Izzy's enthusiasm and her weak smile is soon fully erased by an onset of anxiety. 'Tone. Didn't expect to see you. What's up?'

Tony grins and gathers his daughter into his arms, his rucksack swaying like a counterweight. 'Thought I'd help out. Take this little kitten off your hands.'

'Nah. She's no trouble. Jess not tell you I'm having her after school?'

Tony continues to smile, though it is forced. And when he directs his attention to Penny, whatever mirth was present in his expression as he greeted Izzy is entirely absent. 'Jess forget to tell you that I'm her father?'

'Eh? What you on about?'

Tony turns his back on Penny and beams at his daughter.

'What you say to a McDonalds and some Dad-time?'

'Yes!'

Penny slaps on the pushchair's brakes, glances at the two foundation kids to make sure they're okay, then takes a step towards Tony. 'Hang on, Izz. Tone. No. What you thinking? Come off it. Jess'll—'

'What? She'll what? Make all the decisions, does she? Got you running round for her an' all.'

'It ain't like that. Be reasonable. I'm responsible for—'

'All these other kids.' Tony winks at the two kids who peer back at him nervously. His energy and stance are all wrong, defiant and shifty. 'So don't be greedy. You got enough. This little one is coming with her dad. Women, eh, Izz! Think they got a monopoly.'

'What's monopoly?' Izzy asks while staring at the dressing wrapped around her dad's knuckles.

Penny steps closer and reaches for Izzy. 'Tone. No.'

Tony turns to Penny. Moves fast like a bantamweight boxer, light on his toes. And, for a moment, his grin twists into a nasty sneer and he pushes his forehead far too close to Penny's now fearful face. As their noses almost touch, his hands fist, briefly, before he dances away and offers a high-five to Izzy. 'Come on, kiddo. Let's get some tea. Then we can pick up your mum. She'll be all like, no, no, early night! Cus we been out looking at flats and new schools and God knows what.'

Now mute with fear, Penny backs away. And as Tony saunters off with Izzy holding his hand, she scrabbles inside her bag, looped from the pushchair's handles.

'So what's this new place like, Izz?' Tony asks.

'It's amazing! There's a park!'

33

Shaking from shock after the attack, amidst the cacophony of the bird cries, Jess manoeuvres the wheelchair inside the living room, then swipes open the incoming call on her phone.

'Jess! He took Izzy! Jess, you there?'

Seeking better reception, Jess flits to the hall.

'What you mean, he took Izzy?' Trying to catch her breath, she drifts into the kitchen only to slump against the cupboards.

'Just now. He was up her school. Waiting. He took her.'

Jess closes her eyes to stem the tears that want to break and roll. 'He can't!' Sharpened by anxiety and fear for her daughter, Jess's shrill tone penetrates the living room. Flo sits up straight and turns her head towards the door. Now out of her carer's sight, she wriggles and rocks backwards and forwards like an escapologist freeing herself from ropes or chains.

Penny too is on the verge of tears. 'I know, Jess. But I could hardly stop him. I tried, Jess. But he wouldn't have it. He's a fuck. . . Bully. And he knows, Jess. About your new place. Izz give him the address and everything.'

Jess inhales sharply and drops the phone. She bends over and places her hands upon her thighs, her arms shaking.

She raises the hand she nearly used to strike Flo and stares at it in disbelief. Absentmindedly, she moves the hand to touch the scar on her mouth.

Jess's SOS handset beeps. Her client is on the move again.

Jess retrieves the device from her pocket. The screen indicates that Flo is nearly off the screen.

From her phone, Penny's tiny voice blurts, 'Jess? Jess? Can't hear ya.'

Confused but still alert to crisis, Jess dashes to the hallway so she can peer into the living room. Her vision locks onto Flo's empty wheelchair.

Hands on her cheeks, her eyes stricken with disbelief, she approaches the chair. The restraints are still closed, fastened into loops. The screen of the handset bleeps incessantly as it tracks the rapidly increasing distance between carer and client. A client that Jess cannot see, either in the living room or in what's visible of the garden.

She rushes to the patio doors and peers outside. 'Flo. Flo!'

In response, her client's brittle voice travels from a distance. 'Erce. Erce. Erce.'

Jess's frantic survey seeks the origin of the voice and snags upon a flicker of red amongst the trees of the glade. Flo's dressing gown. 'Christ!' She stumbles from the vicarage to the lawn, runs to the tree-line.

At the fringe of trees guarding the grove and its black reflective heart of water, Jess slows. She's seen this place before but only in dreams. The reality of the pond in the glade is no different to the place she travelled to during sleep. Shards of sunlight spear the foliage and strike the ground. A profound stillness envelopes the sacred space. The distance to the end of the surrounding wood is hard to gauge. The trees appear to march forever. The air and light are ethereal, beautiful, but also forbidding, the atmosphere so uncanny that only a splash of scarlet at the edge of the pond is capable of breaking Jess's bewildered trance.

Hesitantly, she picks her way through the eerily silent trees and draws closer to the still water. She identifies the red garment as Flo's discarded gown. 'Flo?' A red slipper lies beside the gown. Jess peers at the surface of the black water. 'God, no.'

Bubbles pop in the centre of the onyx water, the gentle disturbance sending circles to the surrounding edge. The outermost ripple guides Jess's attention to the second slipper, waterlogged but still bobbing in a bed of reeds.

Too frightened to just wade into the lightless water in which no bottom is visible, she paces the soft shoreline back and forth before forcing herself to enter the pond.

When only knee-deep, the air is knocked from her by the freezing water, the surface reflecting so many trees, the sky, all set to a shimmer by her entrance. She wades on, and sinks to her thighs. The surface rises further, tightening her chest and making her gasp for breath as she stumbles deeper, her body disappearing below the waist. Through her panicked vision, the trees swoop and rotate.

Jess ploughs on, the water rising to her chest. Swishing her arms through the water in the middle, she rakes the lightless depths with her fingers and drags the darkness, seeking the body of her client.

A few feet before her, an eruption of bubbles pulls her eyes to a suggestion of white cloth, barely visible in the murk. Jess heaves herself towards the flotsam, the water swilling under her armpits and shortening her breath even further. She snatches at the submerged fabric, her fingers grasping what resembles a long pale object, perhaps a bony forearm.

The limb seized, she hauls it free of the surface.

Dead wood.

And an old, stained garment is entwined around the blanched tree branch. It's been there for ages but the stick is also caught on, or attached to, something larger. Jess pulls and tugs until the curved side of a vast ball breaks the surface. An intricately woven cage created from sticks and twigs, blackened yet preserved by the peaty water.

Jess backs away from the middle of the pond to the bank, the water's depth decreasing, her legs returning, gleaming and sodden, to the unearthly light of the grove. As she returns to the bank, she continues to haul out the stick-ball. It grows larger as it emerges, and lighter as the water drains from it.

As more of the object appears she recognises the object to be similar to the effigy in the woodcut on the wall of the vicarage's first-floor landing. It is also the thing that was half-made from hawthorn branches in one of the old photos of the women's group in the vicarage garden. The pictures of Flo and her friends in the '70s.

In the shallows, the last of the water pours from the sides of the curious entanglement of sticks until the structure resembles a creel or large basket. Purpose-built, this is some kind of vessel or trap shaped like a beehive. About the ghastly container, rotting clothes are entwined and the quills of long decomposed bird feathers spike.

Jess turns the ball and a crude hole becomes visible, like a porthole wide enough for an occupant to peer out of. She seizes the spokes of the creel and rolls the aperture closer to her face.

Sunlight drops through the hole into the glistening container. Jess's horrified vision follows the light.

A twig-wheel is fixed to the foot of the basket. A withered human hand, cut roughly from an arm, has been spiked into the hub of the spoked circle.

Higher up inside the creel there is a dangling object, a thing dull and glimmering. A skeletal foot.

Bloodless with cold and shock and smeared with grime, Jess's face hitches and her eyelids twitch as if eager to close. Yet still she turns the woven nest to create a new angle to peer through the fissure.

Bound and woven within the interior of the strange twig-ball, more human remains become visible. Like a grub or black larva inside the imprisoning chrysalis of woven sticks hangs the tortured statement of what was once a man, with its genitals removed.

Peat-tanned flesh glistens black and clings to the skeletal remains and contorted face, the teeth and tongue absent from the open maw. The eye sockets are also empty. The figure was mutilated, blinded and castrated, then encased within the hawthorn vessel. Ritual slaughter.

The Vessel

Jess screams and releases the basket. She falls. Pushing
with her feet, then scrabbling, she noisily splashes and claws
her way from the shallows to the mossy floor of the glade
surrounding the black water.

The hideous creel settles into the water but doesn't sink.

Once free of the freezing pond, Jess's hearing is beset anew
by the agitated birds and something far stranger. A distant
bony piping. The woodwind music that she's heard before in
her nightmares. Or are these noises purely within her mind?
She can see no birds, no piper. She clasps her hands to the side
of her head to try and kill her hearing. But her hands fail to
smother the sound of a little girl sobbing among the distant
trees, cries that follow the lonesome notes of the pipe.

From the distance, the doorbell of the vicarage chimes
and resonates through the still air like a church bell.

Too disturbed and witless to react to any of it, Jess can
only shiver and blink. Her face so dirty, her expression a mask
of shock and her hair straggling, she stands up and gapes at
the great old trees of the grove. Turning about, she looks at
the circle of trunks rearing like the columns of an ancient
wooden temple, fashioned around the dark circle of water.
And gradually, as a new perspective takes hold, she detects
a set of faint, ancient tracks, their grooves barely visible as
depressions in the foliage. They spread like spokes from a hub
that is the black pond.

Golden shafts of sunlight carve the air, and – amidst a
tangle of vines, weeds and nettles – the skeleton of a rotten
wooden cart becomes visible, decomposing and returning to
nature. Before she can begin to process what it is that she is
seeing, Jess hears her daughter's voice. From the lawn of the
vicarage, Izzy is now contributing to the pandemonium by
squealing with excitement.

Jess's puzzled reverie is broken. 'Izzy.' Falling about like
a drunkard, she runs from the grove in the direction of the
vicarage, the lawn growing visible through the defensive
palisade of trees.

Behind her fleeing back, the black nest of sticks is dragged into the pond from beneath the surface. But Jess doesn't look back. Nothing matters but reaching her daughter who is inexplicably here, in this mad, sinister place.

And yes, there is Izzy. On the lawn, the vicarage rearing behind her. Sunlight shimmers upon the girl's brushed hair, pulled into the bunches that her mother fashioned that morning and embellished with a pink bow. Definitely Izzy, wearing her school uniform and cartwheeling, perfectly but inexplicably. Cartwheeling like a trained gymnast.

Bewitched by her sudden and uncanny ability to cartwheel, the little girl only glances at the approach of her harassed, grimy, bedraggled mother.

And that's Tony's voice now too! 'All on your own here? Your garage is bigger than most places we lived in.' *He's* here. In the vicarage. And at the sound of her ex's voice barking from out of the French windows, Jess seizes up. 'Three of us and all. That was half the problem. Don't seem right, does it?'

Jess begins to shake. 'Izzy, love?'

'Mummy, watch!'

'Stay here, love. Don't come inside until Mummy says. You hear?'

Jess approaches the open French windows, through which a tale from her ex-husband's tawdry past continues to unfold. 'Assault and battery. Four years in the nick. Four years of her I missed. Too long.'

Speechless with shock, Jess drifts inside the living room and surveys the scene before her.

Tony is sitting in an armchair, a rucksack on his lap. One hand rests protectively upon the bag and fingers the zipper.

Flo sits in her wheelchair. Her feet are filthy. She wears nothing but the white nightgown. But she is completely dry.

Jess glances over her shoulder and into the garden where Izzy is now performing a handstand.

'Bleedin' hell, Jess, what's she got you doing, the gardening and all? You look a right state.'

Jess ignores Tony and slowly walks to the wheelchair. She bends and reattaches the Velcro restraints around each of Flo's wrists and ankles.

Tony laughs derisively. 'Don't think that's necessary. What's she gonna do? Took her half an hour to reach her chair from the front door.'

Jess turns and confronts Tony. 'You can't come here. You've been told. I could lose my job. Another one cus of you.'

From jocular and cocky, Tony's demeanour changes. His whole being grows still and his eyes express a loathing barely tempered by his tight, unpleasant smile. 'But then you always was a control freak.'

From the wheelchair, Flo chimes in and matter-of-factly states, 'He has to go.'

Tony sneers. 'This what you want, Jess, changing some old retard's nappies? Working all hours to scrape enough together to take a little girl away from her dad? What kind of mother are you?'

Jess peers at Flo. 'You let him in.'

Flo smiles sweetly. 'He has to go.'

'Bent over backwards to make things right since I got out. And you was just going to fuck off with Izzy to some new flat without saying a word. You push and you push and you always did. Reached the end of me rope, Jess.'

Flo repeats herself with added emphasis. 'He has to go!'

Tony is up. He leaps at the wheelchair and pushes his face into Flo's. 'Shut it, cunt!'

His raised voice triggers Jess's panic. She doesn't know what to do. Her body begins to shake as if in a prelude to a seizure. She struggles to breathe.

Outside on the lawn, Izzy is inexplicably standing on her head for the first time in her life, smiling and haloed by sunlight. 'Flo! Look! Look! Mummy! Daddy!'

Flo inexplicably and effortlessly slips her hands out of her restraints, as if those lumpy extremities are mice that have flattened their skeletal structures to scurry through a narrow pipe. She raises those old hands above the chair's armrests and rotates her wrists so that her hands depict twin wheel sigils in the air before her, rolling anticlockwise.

Tony steps away from the wheelchair and turns to the garden. When he catches sight of his deliriously happy daughter, tears fill his eyes. From rage to love. Just as quickly, his expression blanks again as instability and a powerful internal maelstrom resume their hold. When he returns to Jess, his face is bloodless and moist with sweat, his expression tense, committed.

Jess backs away. 'You can't come near either of us.'

Tony pounces and seizes Jess's arm. She flinches, cowers down, her hands protecting her scarred mouth. 'Don't. Please, Tony. Don't.'

Tony's enraged face closes. One fist is clenched and he's struggling to restrain himself. He drags Jess across to his rucksack. When he unclenches his fist he dips that hand inside the bag and withdraws a length of coloured cord. And a knife. 'If I ain't having her, you ain't either. There's another way for us all to be together.'

They stare at each other and Jess at once recognises the terrible purpose in Tony's eyes. She swallows and shakes her head and whispers, 'No. Tone. No.'

'It's that time, love. We're there now. All of us. You brought us here.'

Flo begins to rock back and forth while staring intently at nothing in the room. At the end of her extended arms, her hands open and her palms turn to face the ceiling. 'Erce. Erce. Erce.'

Tony releases Jess's arm, turns and slaps Flo's old head hard. 'Fuck off, I said! Fucking die already! Bitch!'

Jess is on her feet and running from the room.

Tony glances at the garden where oblivious Izzy capers and cartwheels delightedly. Then he turns and pursues Jess.

Jess arrives at the front door and yanks the handle. It won't open because Tony has already put the catch on and locked them all inside. She futilely slaps a hand against the door then turns and races into the dead-end of the darkened dining room.

Tony strides across the hallway. Behind him, in the distant living room, Flo's freed hands draw a bigger circle anticlockwise. And above Tony's head, the new light bulb implodes.

He flinches. 'The fuck!' Then returns his attention to Jess in the dining room. 'Get here! Now!'

Jess drops to her knees and attempts to crawl inside the tunnel that burrows amidst the furniture and boxes stacked around the dining table.

Tony slaps on the overhead light.

BANG! A second light bulb explodes above his head. He flinches then looks at the fitting, unnerved but too enraged to stop. 'Fuckin' 'ell! You brought our daughter here an' all! To a death trap to wipe up a spaz's dribble!' He races to the mouth of the tunnel and grabs Jess's ankles. Yanks her backwards, out and onto the floor.

CRACK! A stack of old boxes near the mouth of the tunnel collapses against Tony's head. 'Cunt!' Tony throws the obstacles aside. A hurled box smashes against the dining room wall. 'Whole place is falling apart. And you bring our child here. As a mother, you are shite! You always was.' Tony grasps Jess's ankles and drags her backwards from the room.

Jess waves her arms around, trying to hold onto anything to moor herself. But Tony kicks and shoves any articles away from her grasping hands. As if she is a wheelbarrow pulled in reverse, he drags her backwards through the room, face down. Out and into the hall.

'God, no! God, no. Tony! Stop! Think of Izzy!'

Tony hauls Jess across the hallway and back into the living room and up to his rucksack and the rope and the knife, then releases her legs.

Jess turns over, pulls her top down, struggles to her knees and sobs. She looks to the garden to make sure Izzy won't see what's about to happen to her mum.

Izzy prances happily about the lawn. Skip, skip, skip, cartwheel!

Jess turns to face Tony, who looms above her. He wipes at the blood that seeps from under his hair where a heavy box cracked his head in the dining room. 'Tone. No. We can all be together in the new place. It's for us. All of us. Real family home.'

'Liar!' Tony swings. A sickening meaty thud booms through the living room and Jess is back down flat, her mouth split apart. The scar reopened.

Tony's face is contorted by animal rage as he raises a fist above his stricken, cowering ex-wife, so huddled into herself and dazed. But he pauses and his next blow is not delivered. He looks up instead, and his anger immediately drains into a surprise that transforms just as quickly into disbelief. 'The fuck?'

Against the sun-bright French windows, and within that rectangle of celestial light, Flo hovers in mid-air. Above the wheelchair an aged woman levitates. Head tilted back like a baby bird about to receive something between its stretched jaws, Flo's mouth is a black hole. Her throat moves as if she's gulping at the air, yet the client makes no sound. Her aged arms and lumpy hands are raised palm upwards.

A cloud passes over the house and douses the sun's glare. The colour of Flo's face darkens. As do her limbs, until they appear even more horribly stick-like, completing her transformation into a blackened and terrible spectacle. As if the new darkness is spreading outwards from the shadow that transforms Flo, the very room dims to its corners. When Flo speaks it is Tony's voice that barks from her withered mouth. 'He broke your teeth, bitch!'

Turning owl-like, Flo's head swivels to stare at Jess. With her hair so wild, the client resembles a mad conductor whose hands have risen to draw the highest note from an orchestra.

Jess rises to her feet in one unnaturally swift movement, a floppy marionette pulled erect by the puppet-master and made rigid once more.

Flo drops her hands and Jess is released from the force that held her and dragged her upright. Mouth bleeding heavily and eyes frantic with terror and disbelief, when she regains her feet and balance, she staggers sideways and nearer to the fireplace.

Tony remains still and agape below the monstrous elderly figure hovering in thin air.

Jess finds and meets Flo's infernally white eyes. The stare is held and a moment of understanding passes between the two women.

Jess steps to the fireplace and snatches up the barbed iron poker.

Flo speaks again. In Tony's voice. 'Pulled your hair out! Spat in your fucking face!'

Tony totters, paralysed by the suspension of reason and natural law within the living room. He's stricken by hearing his own voice continue to issue from the aged form hovering in thin air. He can only blink in wonder and horror at Flo.

As if within a solar eclipse, Jess is briefly silhouetted against the windows overlooking the garden and she also grows as dark as her client. Her eyes and her teeth in that bloodied mouth are white and wild and horrid against the shadowy surround of her face. From her hand, a weapon protrudes.

A mother cornered, her child threatened, Jess twists around, the speed of her movement startling. Unleashing a primal, inhuman shriek, she whips the poker into Tony's head, hard. Flesh and bone absorb the impact, producing a sickening thud.

Jess's face quivers. Her eyes possess a malevolence unbearable to look upon for long. She swings the poker again, from the waist, throwing her entire back and shoulders into the blow.

A dull coconutting sound ends wetly inside the living room.

And again, this blackened and dreadful mother swings the poker. And again. And again. And again. Her facial expression and her eyes do not alter. Red suds fly from the poker and decorate the white ceiling.

Outside in the dreamy sun-drenched garden, Izzy continues to cartwheel, turning a circle across the lawn. As if functioning as her audience, the birds cry out joyously.

Each *thwack* from inside the vicarage, as Izzy's mother smashes apart her father's head as if it is a melon, can be heard outside. But the moist smacks are mostly obscured by the ecstatic chorus of the birds. Bewitched and enraptured by the miracle of her new gymnastic prowess, Izzy ignores the distant noise of butchery. But if the little girl had cast her eyes towards the living room, on the other side of those French doors she would have seen her mother and Flo obscured by shadows. Yet, despite the gloom, her mother would have appeared darker and thinner than she ever could be normally. From within the gloom, her mother's eyes and teeth would have shone back at her too, gleaming yellow-white as she HAMMERS the old iron poker DOWN onto Daddy's head, again and again and again and again. Until all that her mother is striking is the very floor of Nerthus House.

When the violent moment has passed and her work is done, and she has made sure that she has been thorough and she can barely raise her arms, Jess staggers out of the diminishing, shrinking shadow that was so recently upon this room. Gasping with exhaustion, her posture wilting to a slouch, she casts aside the dripping poker and turns her stricken face, blood-flecked with gruesome graffiti, to the garden.

'Mummy, look what I can do!'

Flo is returned to her carriage as if she'd never left it. But she too is spent. Old and depleted and near extinguished by her own exertions. Her head has fallen across her chest, her arms and legs hang lifelessly.

Jess sways to her client and drops. She kneels before the chair like a supplicant before a throne. With one hand, she raises Flo's aged head. And she finds that Flo's eyes are sparkling with love. The old woman looks at Jess in the same way she first regarded Izzy. A knowing smile plays about the sunken mouth.

'You . . .' Jess says, but doesn't know how to finish the thought. She points instead at the window and in the direction of the grove and those distant columns of trees crowning the garden. 'That . . . thing. Up there. In the sticks. Your husband. You did that.'

Flo responds with silence but maintains her knowing smile. Serene now, the old woman appears to have arrived at a curious peace.

Jess wipes at her own tears that dribble into the blood shining upon her mouth and chin. 'All of it. You. From when I showed up. Was you.'

Flo turns her head and smiles sweetly at Izzy in the garden. 'Isn't she adorable.' The old woman's expression is calm and kind. A benign dementia patient once again. Sunlight washes through the room as if black clouds have drifted from across a glorious sun. Melodic birdsong pierces and enlivens the room, banishing the forbidding atmosphere that so recently reigned here. A startling moment of clarity surfaces in Flo's expression and her eyes moisten. 'My little birds have flown, Jessica.'

Jess starts. It is the first time she has heard her client say her name.

Tears break and run down her client's ancient, anguished face. 'Did you want to sit in my chair?'

Jess drops her face to the frail sticks of her client's thighs. She sobs hard, her entire body wracked with shudders. Coming down. Coming down hard from being electrified. Coming down fast from the terrible impact of what she has just done and been consumed by. Her whole body tries to shake itself apart. And yet she extends her arms around her client like a child reaching for its mother.

Flo gently places one hand upon the back of her carer's head and looks at the window, seeking and finding happy frolicking Izzy upon the lawn, the sunlight out there so bright. Flo strokes Jess's hair and whispers. 'They're everything. Always.'

SCRICK! comes the sound of a key thrust into the front door.

34

*D*amp, bedraggled, her clothing stained and hair hanging about her face, her mouth bleeding and her ex-husband dead upon the floor with a catastrophic head injury, Jess stands beside Flo's chair, resigned, if she can even feel that much.

Scowling, put-upon, loaded down with carrier bags, Morag ambles and slouches into the living room. She eyes Tony's corpse and ponders the crushed skull and terrible glistening stain. And shrugs nonchalantly. 'About bleedin' time, you ask me.'

Jess stares at the night worker as if at a traffic accident. An eyelid twitches before she blinks rapidly, attempting to comprehend her colleague's reaction.

Morag drops her bags. Wasting no time, she seizes Tony's lifeless ankles and drags his inert form out of the living room, pulling the corpse in a series of jerks, grunting as she moves. Above his lifeless body, her teeth are set in a grimace from exertion, or even satisfaction. It's hard to tell.

Morag's retreating form incrementally dissolves to a black silhouette. The sun strikes and illumines the spoked wheel of the stained glass above the front door. A colourful eye.

Tony's corpse is tugged onwards and to the tunnel in the dining room where Jess discovered the first shrine, the first stick-wheel. His crimson, misshapen head leaks horribly. His arms are cast out upon the old, threadbare carpet but away he goes to the dusty articles of furniture, boxes, bags, books.

Morag ducks down, crawls backwards into the dark aperture of the tomb within this room, until her body disappears entirely. Her two fleshy arms then thrust out and seize Tony's ankles.

His body, in a final series of jerks, is yanked completely into the darkness. Once his remains are entirely ensconced inside the tunnel, Morag chuckles to herself.

Hands planted on either side of the kitchen sink, Jess barks the meagre contents of her stomach into the empty basin, then gasps for air.

Dropping her head upon the metal draining board, she sees the room from an angle, her head on one side. Around her, the fixtures sparkle after their recent thorough clean. She grasps the clean tea towel she's wrapped around a bag of frozen peas and stuffs it against her leaking mouth. Just as she did so many years ago when her child was a toddler and screamed from her walker in the mouth of the kitchen as her mother scrabbled to retrieve her broken teeth from the floor. But she cannot dwell on that because, outside the vicarage, the movement in the street catches her eye.

Bathed by the sun's radiance, a group of elderly women stand at the foot of the front path. Flo's neighbours. The constant gardener wearing the sun hat, the two dog walkers, the two other elderly ladies that Jess glimpsed behind dim windows. So proud of her, they all sweetly beam at Jess. Parked behind their backs is her boss's car. Beside the vehicle stands Sheila but as Jess has never seen her before. No longer stern of face and mean of spirit, her manager smiles at her employee and even touches the corner of one eye. She's so proud of Jess, so happy for her.

The eyes of the elderly neighbour who spoke to Jess are shielded once more by the wide brim of a sun hat but the lower half of her face is broken by a broad smile that reveals her strong white teeth. In one hand she holds a polished, short-handled scythe. Though it's the same size as the one that hangs upon the vicarage wall, this is a newer, sharper model and its cruel blade glints in the sun-blessed air, ready for use.

Their faces gleeful, Sheila and the five elderly women all raise one hand simultaneously. Each lifted hand is clad in a rubber glove as if they have arrived to clean the vicarage. They all mark the air with a closing circle at the same time, then cross their circles with spokes.

Beside them in the street, stands a large wheelbarrow. Upon it, the hump of a spherical man-sized creel, constructed from hawthorn sticks.

Like a confused, elderly woman, Jess teeters from the kitchen. With the tea towel pressed against her mouth, she hands herself through the hall and into the living room. Behind her, the front door admits the coven.

Morag's heavy feet are planted on a large throw rug that covers the bloodstains and other matter that had scattered from Tony's smashed head. All of it is now concealed. The poker has gone.

Morag smiles at Jess and the night carer's eyes are lit with pleasure. It's the first time she's appeared genuinely happy, or even so much as warmed to Jess. 'Blossom gonna sleep beautifully now. Better than she's known in a very long time.'

Izzy capers into the living room from the garden and kneels before Flo's chair. She smiles at the elderly woman. Though exhausted, Flo still manages to rest a gnarled hand upon the little girl's head and she gazes into the child's eyes lovingly.

Izzy glances at her mother on the far side of the room. 'Where's Dad?'

'He had to go,' Flo whispers.

Jess swallows and attempts a pained smile with what can be seen of her mouth behind the towel. 'Yes, love. He had to go.'

'Mummy, your mouth is hurt.'

Haggard and bewildered, Jess totters and sways gently, barely keeping it together. 'It's all right, luv. Just banged it helpin' Flo.'

Flo's worn face and moist eyes turn to look into the light falling from the garden. And she smiles. Reflected upon the pupil of her rheumy eye, Charlotte Gardner, aged around seven, plays out there. Dressed in the very outfit Izzy wore when sleepwalking, Charlotte cartwheels, hair flying, her juvenile limbs flashing an arc. When her routine ends and she stands tall, she flings her arms into the air. A young gymnast performing for an audience.

Directing her lovely smile at the house, she's so pleased with herself and now seeks approval from the watcher at the window. Behind her, a solemn unsmiling boy stands self-consciously and watches the girl. Who cartwheels twice more. Turning through the air, her image begins to flicker then grow indistinct. Fading to monochrome until the joyous, innocent, tumbling girl and the watching boy disintegrate. Are gone.

Morag moves to Flo and takes Flo's free hand. They look deeply into each other's eyes. Flo nods and Morag turns to Jess, her eyes shining. 'Jess. Take Flo to her room.'

35

The five elderly neighbours stand with Sheila and Morag beneath the stained glass fanlight. Their heads are bowed as if before a queen. Queen Flo, a shrunken, near lifeless figure that Jess carries in her arms like a child to the foot of the stairs. A sombre Izzy follows without fully grasping what is going on.

Up the stairs they go. The young mother and carer carrying the old mother to her bed. A little girl, the next generation, following and blissfully innocent of all that has happened this day.

Behind them in the hall, the scythe in the neighbour's gloved hand catches the light and flashes like a precious metal.

As Flo and her entourage disappear, the neighbours, Morag and Sheila file into the dining room where Tony's body lies hidden. Their work is about to begin.

Bedclothes seal Flo's lower body and legs. Her two thin arms lie upon the covers. A small regal bird. Her thinning hair is brushed up and back from her forehead like a crown. Her motionless, unblinking eyes are open and she watches the window, her expression peaceful.

Jess and Izzy lie on the bed, on either side of Flo. Izzy, her face tear-stained, sniffles. Flo and Jess each hold one of Izzy's little hands.

All of the windows are wide open. Sunlight blesses the room, giving it the appearance of a celestial chamber. Outside, a distant murmur of voices rises from the garden.

Izzy raises her head to look at old Flo. 'Flo? Flo? Mummy?'

Jess drops Flo's cupped hand and examines the thin wrist for a pulse while watching the elderly face closely. 'Flo?'

Her client has passed away. Jess swallows and places Flo's hand alongside her body, then sits up as Morag enters the room respectfully, drying her hands on a towel stained reddish. 'She's gone.'

Jess nods her bemused assent. Wistful yet satisfied that all is in order, Morag moves round the bed and strokes Izzy's hair. 'Blossom said it was gonna be soon. She only hung on for you.'

From the distance, a familiar name is called by a chorus of elderly voices. 'Erce. Erce. Erce.'

Jess turns her head and follows Flo's dead gaze to the window. She slips off the bed and walks to the golden window, blazing with light.

At the edge of the grove, at the peak of the expansive garden, there is movement. And of a type to make Jess catch her breath.

Sheila and a small group of elderly figures, their arms and clothing stained blood-red like butchers, move along the tree-lined edge of the grove. Unsteadily, four of them push the large wheelbarrow. A hand-drawn vehicle containing the hive-shaped structure woven from sticks. The vessel when empty weighs little but when filled with the grisly cargo it was designed to carry, it requires a cart.

At the rear, as if in a trance, Sheila walks as slowly as an undertaker behind a hearse. Her eyes are closed. Out in front of the group, the elderly neighbour in the sun hat leads the way, waving the soiled scythe before her and clearing the ground of nettles and other impediments. The ensemble haltingly makes its way towards the black iridescence of the grove's heart, the pond.

Deeper inside, beside the water, what resembles the tall trunk of a slender black tree subtly moves itself in absolute silence. A long, though vague, form with a narrow, beaked head. It passes through the far-off boughs and vanishes into darkness.

Jess turns from the window, her expression transfixed again by the shock of what the vicarage is making her confront. She looks to the bed and at Flo's lifeless body beneath the covers, the open eyes staring directly into the light. Jess looks to Morag. 'What is it?'

'Mother. Goddess. They're still in some places. Groves. That's one.' Morag then nods her world-weary head to Jess. 'Looks like we's out of a job. Come on, let's call ambulance for Blossom.'

Out there, beyond the garden, a new sound seeps from the distant grove. The noise of an object being pulled into a body of water and dragged down. The submersion is followed by joyous cries, a chorus of women.

36

Months later, and Izzy is playing on the grass of the vicarage lawn again. She's positioning a new collection of the big-eyed soft toys that she coveted in the supermarket. They form a ring about the cat toy that her father gave her.

The little blonde girl, whom Jess once saw waving goodbye to her grandmother who lives across the street, sits beside Izzy, intent on a game that transfixes them.

On a blanket laid out upon the lush grass, Jess sits near the girls. A new haircut frames her face, which is finally more than relaxed – perhaps even serene. Through the lenses of her sunglasses she surveys her happy daughter with evident pleasure, then opens an elegant hamper and removes food for a picnic. She lays these treats upon the blanket for the girls.

'What about tomorrow?' asks Izzy's new friend.

Without looking up from the toys, Izzy answers her friend. 'It'll be sunny. We'll be out tomorrow.'

Jess turns and looks at her new neighbour, crowned as ever with her distinctive sun hat and busy at work with freshly cut flowers.

'How long you staying?' Izzy's little friend asks her.

'Oh, we live here now. Flo give the house to your nanna. And she give it us.'

The gardener approaches the picnic blanket bearing colourful gifts: floral tiaras, one for each girl, one for Jess.

'And this will be a happy place again, protecting all who love her.'

Subtly, Jess raises a single hand into the air and discreetly makes Flo's sign, the sign of the Eadric villagers. A closed circle. Beside her, the two little girls don't notice.

A bird alights from the yew tree beside the group and bursts into the air. The vicarage and the garden grow smaller below its ascent. As the bird flies higher, the earth takes on the shape of a new pattern. An eye. In the centre of a bushy copse of tree tops resembling a rough green iris, the tiny black pond of the grove becomes a pupil staring into the sky. From out of the fringe of greenery that is the grove, the faint lines of ancient green paths form spokes that pass in straight lines from the pond. They reach beyond the boundary of the vicarage and thread between the tiny buildings of Eadric.

From so far up, the pond and protective grove become the tiny dark hub of a vast spoked wheel that reaches beyond the outer buildings of the village. And if there is a wheel-rim it is visible as that ancient track, or earthwork, so far below, encircling and protecting the old settlement. The same shape as the twig-wheels found within the vicarage shrines. The same shape as the stained glass fanlight above the front door of Nerthus House. An old wheel.

Story Notes:
About This Horror

*A*fter *The Ritual* was adapted into a film at the end of 2016, I thought seriously about writing a screenplay for a horror film. The production of *The Ritual* gave me a meaningful insight into a four-year development of a feature film: how the business of filmmaking erects its pyramids, how a screenplay is produced on the creative side, how directors are sourced and chosen, films cast, locations scouted, sets built, productions organised around shooting scripts. I watched with fascination, plenty of disbelief and some awe.

It's so hard to get these expensive entities made; so much can go wrong, so much does go wrong, so many people are involved, moving parts all move at the same time, the variables are bewildering, the stakes and deadlines are terrifying once the trigger is pulled. And then post-production can seem interminable. Why go through it?

I ask the same of people who climb mountains. But then, if you think about it, nothing worth doing is easy. But that view from the summit, and that intense, euphoric feeling of being transported by a film on a screen, becomes the equivalent of a city of gold that drove the Spaniards mad in South America. The madness is a virus, contagious, and I caught it too. Why not me? I asked myself. Why not join the expedition into the jungle? I have good boots.

Prior to this, screenwriting was something ephemeral to my eye, alchemical, requiring special techniques and knowledge and expertise that I lacked. No one had ever asked me to write a screenplay. I took that for a show of no confidence. After all of these novels, stories and a few awards, I wasn't even on the bench: I was in the stands. A spectator.

But, for years, most of my books had gone in and out of development and I'd read treatments, the odd screenplay, attended meetings but most often sat through 18-month silences with nothing happening. Films weren't made and options elapsed or passed into other hands. Things may have happened during these silent intervals but I was on the outside of this mystical realm of films and their people. Not so with *The Ritual* – I was kept in the loop. I saw it happen.

I've dedicated my adult life, from my mid-teens onwards, to the book, primarily the novel. That was what I have always been about; writing books became the purpose of my everyday when still at school. Pulling that off is a sufficient challenge for one lifetime. And yet I was a lover of film and had been watching horror films for a long time before I made the move from being a reader of horror to a writer of it.

I eventually realised that my vocation for the novel was good training, because my focus was stories, and making horror work within those stories. Whether the stories are long or short or in between, the ultimate aesthetic goals are the same, and the story and horror need to entwine and work together. I'd been schooled in foreboding, tension and creating set pieces. Surely I could transfer these to a script? In my head, at least, all of my stories had been films anyway, so what I needed to do was study the techniques, formats and process of writing a screenplay, before writing one.

This is why there was no book from me in 2018. I went back to school. Took a sabbatical, all on my own.

I'd managed a book each year since 2010. One year, 2017, two were published. But as I rewrote *The Reddening* across

2017 and 2018, I studied screenplays in between drafts of the novel and had a go at writing one in 2018 – *The Vessel*. Then a second screenplay in 2019 (*Cunning Folk*), and a third in 2020.

At the risk of repeating the story notes at the rear of *Cunning Folk*, by the time I had completed my research, written loglines and treatments, then moved on to first drafts of the 110-page screenplays, in each case I'd acknowledged a few things. Chiefly, the screenplays will, statistically and in all probability, never become films. At the time of writing, all three are in some form of development and the screenplays have been produced, but none of them are actual films. Yet. But so engaged had I become by the stories and ideas, and the characters that I knew from their secret thoughts and internal organs to their speech patterns and outer layers of skin, I knew these screenplays simply HAD to become novels. There wasn't a doubt in my mind. And what an antidote to the utter futility of writing speculative screenplays these novels have become. The stories live!

With the exception of actors, I think I feel more sympathy and quiet horror for screenwriters than I do for any other creative type. Reaching the goal of an actual film on a screen is nigh on impossible. The years, even decades, they go through, endlessly revising their work as directors come and go, as producers change their minds, as the trigger is nearly pulled before the safety goes back on for another few years... But when a film is actually made, even flying feels possible. Finally, everything makes sense and all is right with the world and the mystical city of gold is something you are inside, actually touching the walls. You got a key!

Staying inside is another matter altogether. But, hey, quite simply, we all want to do and be what we love and admire. It's why so many readers now have 'author' after their name. I'd hazard a guess that there are as many writers now as there are readers. People have to try to do what they love.

And here we are. *The Vessel* was my first screenplay and is now my eleventh novel. The cycle is complete. Including the publishing of this book, *The Vessel* has been on my desk and in my thoughts, in various forms, for five years. So why is it so short?

The answer lies in *Cunning Folk*. That was a difficult book to write, even though I had a fully formed screenplay that had directors and a production company immediately attached to it. *Cunning Folk* I entirely transformed from a screenplay into a novel; entirely, because in the novel almost all of the story is told in very immediate points-of-view within the heads of three characters. You simply cannot do that in a film. You can suggest the inner lives and turmoil of characters in films, through what they say, how they act and react. But you don't know for sure what's going on inside. Not how they feel, exactly. Not what they are thinking, precisely. Flashback and prologues must be used sparingly or not at all. So it's hard to get across what happened to these characters before the action of the film.

Reading fiction, you don't have these problems. You go inside a character. You go deep. Nor is the writer hobbled by a 110-page limit. A reader takes a seat inside a character's head and peers through their eyes and rifles through their back stories in ways you never can as a viewer of a film.

The novel of *Cunning Folk* also became a literary exploration of the inherent mystery of the wild, of landscape, of how the exterior world affects the interior world. By the time I'd finished the novel, I hadn't given the screenplay a thought in a couple of years. In fact, I didn't give the screenplay any thought when I began the novel. The break between the two mediums was total and complete, aesthetically. One is a screenplay; the other is an original novel, not tie-in fiction. The story structure is near identical but the execution and scope of each are worlds apart. Same story with vastly different forms, preoccupations, textures, styles and remits. If someone else was to adapt the novel into another screenplay,

I'll warrant it'd bear scant resemblance to my screenplay. I'm a novelist and I reverted to following the neural pathways required for me to write a story at novel-length. One hundred and ten pages? To hell with that!

Which left me wondering if that divide between a novel and a screenplay could be narrowed next time around. Could more of a cinematic sense be retained in the adaptation of a script to prose novel? So, with the adaptation of screenplay to novel of *The Vessel*, I tried something new.

In *The Vessel* I removed the interior of the characters.

I'm a bugger for this, I know. I even produced a collection of stories without characters (*Wyrd and Other Derelictions*). So thank you all for your patience and willingness to give my new books a chance and to follow my digressions. My premise for this book was so remarkably simple that I wondered if I was kidding myself about it actually working as a novel. And I might still be.

Chiefly, if a screenplay and, therefore, a film are composed of what is seen by the viewer and what is heard (dialogue, etc.) – and I've read that our experience of films comprises about nine parts what we see or are shown, and one part what is said by the characters – then what would a novel be like if all of the character interior was cut out? So, in effect, the reader only sees what the characters see, and hears what they say, as in a film; but is never, or very rarely, allowed inside their minds, save for one or two moments that would be flashback onscreen. What if the sets and locations are depicted with a brevity similar to the length of a scene in a script (and scenes are not very long – one page of a script equates roughly to one minute of screen-time), and not built in detail over many pages? My structural goal was to turn the scenes of the novel in a similar fashion to the turning of scenes cinematically – becoming as much film editor as novel author.

What was extraordinary, but hardly surprising, was the resulting word count. By my remaining outside my characters' heads and hearts, the novel was reduced to one third of the length of my shortest novel to date, and one fifth of my longest novel. The process was akin to being engaged in the most extreme editing while at the same time writing the first draft.

The process had parallels with rewriting a screenplay, after receiving notes from the director and producers. It is a brutal process and technique must be precise. That 110-page (or fewer) count must be preserved, while maintaining each turn and beat in all the right places, from scene to scene and act to act, while making seismic upheavals in structure. If you want to learn about storytelling, get a screenplay into development. It's a remarkable fast-track experience and nothing else will bring you closer to a stroke, or a scream of animal rage. One's emotions and even instincts must be overruled.

And yet I've been totally engaged writing screenplays. Have really taken to the craft, and I believe it has made me a better storyteller.

I was discussing the writing and publishing of modern genre novels with a friend and correspondent recently. And I was struck again by the notion that using fewer words, primarily less description and less character interior, tends to move readers through stories faster. And is a style favoured by modern commercial publishers. To my eye, this is how 'plot-driven' fiction is written. There are exceptions, particularly in novels that require extensive world-building, but generally, in the age of the thriller, I feel the writing is simpler and more direct. Some might say less sophisticated. But it suits modern tastes, attention spans, leisure time, travel, technology, not least audiobooks, even standards of literacy. It also reveals the emphasis, nigh on tyranny, of plot and story and the demotion of all else. It is the way things are. Literary, lyrical, philosophical, poetic styles and approaches are in decline; story-driven fiction is dominant. And, in my defence when making these sweeping generalisations, as an editor I sat in publishing meetings for eleven years (in the age of the sales director).

To make either approach work well, however, involves considerable feats of skill from a writer; each approach to fiction is faced with remarkable challenges. But the former has a better chance of publication and finding a readership. It also produces more terrible books than should have ever existed. Though, when done well, story-driven books are sublime. When I came across a great commercial book as an editor, and it didn't often happen, I almost wept with joy. The approach is also more cinematic in structure and execution. I see a connection there, at a time when the lithographic plays second fiddle to the pictorial – or what we see on our screens.

But I would also suggest that more elaborate literary styles have a far greater chance of transporting the reader, if the reader has patience. The quality of the writing is closer to poetry. To my eye, it is why the stories of Machen, Blackwood, James (both of them), Lovecraft, Onions, Poe, Jackson, Shelley, Aickman, Campbell, King, Simmons, Barker, Sarah Waters and so many others in the field will endure for longer and resonate more profoundly down the ages. At least for a while, though who knows what will endure if, against all the odds, civilisation survives for a few more centuries. Our relationship with language, and use of it, is always changing. There is no better demonstration of this than the modern novel and the way that it is written. Nor should we forget how many people favour the story-driven approach to fiction that relies upon simpler language and more tension to drive the story and reader forward.

To my eye, I've always attempted to combine the two approaches – the story-driven fiction that I love, and the literary styles that I adore. Many of my favourite novels marry the two approaches. It's never been an either/or argument for me, or for many other writers. You can do both. Eventually, I'd like to think the two aims will come together seamlessly in my own work. My enduring goal: the books will be strange but they will be readable and compelling stories driven by dramatic tension.

I digress. *The Vessel* is an attempt to tighten the relationship between the screen and page, the screenplay and novel, and I wanted the story to feel both cinematic and literary. I've never written anything like this before. I'd hope the book could be finished by a reader in one or two sittings. And I can only hope a reader will be drawn into the situation and will continue reading until the critical mass of the third act, when all hope seems lost for Jess and Izzy. Even though I give the reader a lot less to go on than I usually do in a novel, I can only hope I did my bit well enough. Same deal with the *Derelictions*, I don't want the reader to be conscious that they are reading an experiment (this is why story notes should go at the back) but to enter the story and accept it quickly. I don't want much, do I?

The story is also another block horror – limited locations and cast. Claustrophobic, intense relationships. The situation, though initially simple, had to begin with the stakes raised for Jess, the principal character. She's like many women out there: broke but working hard and a single parent. She's also a victim of domestic violence and afraid of her ex-husband, who's manipulative, persistent and controlling. She has a lovely daughter she can barely provide for who is being bullied at school. But if she can keep this gruelling and under-appreciated gig-economy job going, balancing pennies with child-minders, she can get them out of an awful situation and into a new flat. A new future. She can almost taste it. But everything is going to get so much worse and she could lose far more than her future plans. She could lose her mind, her daughter and her life . . . by taking the job she desperately needs.

Tony won't go away and her new client is disturbed and verbally and physically abusive. The woman's house is a half-lit minefield of horror and decay, lost in the shadow of the worst kind of tragedy any parent can face, in which something really sinister may also have happened. And let's not forget a suggestion of the numinous. That's just the first act. It wasn't easy to show all of that in twenty-six pages in a screenplay format. Compression: what I learned about compression in the screenplay served me well with this novel.

And so far, the book has had three very good young directors come and go onto other things, and they all made a contribution to the story. A fourth who considered the job made a startling observation in a meeting about a plot hole. The producer, Will, pitched in constantly. The first two directors wanted Tony to appear more sympathetic, and rightly too. They also had me going back at this, again and again, to get Jess on night shifts, so my daylight scenes became night-time scenes. The scene with the neighbour who imparts the house's back story, plus enigma, nearly broke me. Izzy's experience in the school outbuilding mirrored a place in the producer's childhood. So, the story was collaborative – it had several editors, more or less – and for a long time after draft five, I couldn't bear to reopen the screenplay. For a novelist with a well-developed internal editor, development within a group can be anathema. I didn't come from a background of workshopping stories: I've always worked alone, or with one editor. But, you learn, you adapt. Mercifully, I've never closed myself off to new ways of writing or publishing. And, hey, even though I am fifty-two (at the time of writing this), I don't think I'm too old to get into this script game either.

We'll see. Meantime, thank you for getting this far and I hope you enjoyed this ritual . . . I mean story.

Manes exite paterni
Adam L. G. Nevill
November 2021, Devon.

Acknowledgements

esearch for *The Vessel* was lengthy, and *Pagan Britain* by Ronald Hutton, *The Lost Gods of England* by Brian Branston, *Looking for the Lost Gods of England* by Kathleen Herbert and *Magical Knowledge: Book 1 Foundations* by Josephine McCarthy enriched the story's background. *The Vessel* also began life as a screenplay, one I developed with Will Tennant and Elisa Scuba, and with Andy and Ryan Tohill in 2018. Their guidance and suggestions were invaluable. Thea Hvistendahl spotted the plot hole.

The Ritual Limited team came through yet again in our goal to produce quality editions in each format. My wife, Anne, packed and shipped all 600 copies of *Cunning Folk* and will have to navigate the same obstacles, and put in the same hours, for *The Vessel*. She also manages the website and accounts and is an excellent proofreader, who proofreads the first proofreader's proofs. Her mother, Gill Parry, then proofreads Anne's version. It never ends!

Samuel Araya again produced fabulous cover art and The Dead Good Design Company designed the jackets for all four editions, as well as every generation of text design. Tony Russell proved indispensable again as the editor of this book (and every other Ritual Limited title), as did Eleanor Abraham as proofreader. TJI printed the hardbacks to a high spec' once more. Amazon and Ingram print the paperbacks and Amazon also remains my primary retailer for the mass-market editions.

Adam L. G. Nevill

I also want to acknowledge the work, much beyond expectation, of Dave, our postmaster, Helen McQueen and We Can Creative for my website and apps. Special mentions are long overdue for long-time support and signal boosts from Kevin Dixon, Ramsey Campbell, Tim Lebbon, Glen Mazarra, Mark Edwards, Cristina Rodlo, Netflix, all at Imaginarium, Alison Flood and the *Guardian*, *Bloody Disgusting*, *Horror D.N.A.*, Daniel Kraus, *Gingernuts of Horror*, Andy Serkis, Paul Finch, David Bruckner, Santiago Menghini, Buccheim Verlag and Cemetery Dance Germany, Astrel in Russia, Trevor Kennedy, Gerard Torbitt, The Shorley, English Riviera UNESCO Global Geopark, Torbay Culture, Writers on the Riviera, Brian J. Showers and Swan River Press, *Lit Reactor*, *The Lineup*. And a big salute to Peter Walters, who narrated the *Cunning Folk* audiobook.

My sincerest thanks go out to the reviewers who supported *Cunning Folk*, not least Jim Moon at *Hypnogoria*, James Grainger of the *Toronto Star*, Paul Holmes and *The Eloquent Page*, Sadie 'Mother Horror' Hartmann and Ashley 'Spookish Mommy' of *Nightworms*, Janine Pipe and *Cemetery Dance*, Gavin Kendall, Steve Stred and Simon Paul Wilson at Kendall Reviews, Joe Scipioni at *Horror Bound*, Tony Jones at *Gingernuts of Horror*, Anthony Watson at *Dark Musings*, Michael Wilson, Bob Pastorella at *This Is Horror*, Janelle Janson at *She Reads with Cats*, Mers of *Harpies in the Trees*, *Read by Dusk*, Simon Avery, *Marc's World of Books* and the many other generous and avid readers and reviewers of my horrors at Instagram and elsewhere online.

Finally, my thanks to all readers of *The Vessel*. The entire ritual of writing these horrors and publishing them would be futile without you. You all remain the most important people in the room.

About the Author

*A*dam L. G. Nevill was born in Birmingham, England, in 1969 and grew up in England and New Zealand. He is an author of horror fiction. Of his novels, *The Ritual*, *Last Days*, *No One Gets Out Alive* and *The Reddening* were all winners of The August Derleth Award for Best Horror Novel. He has also published three collections of short stories, with *Some Will Not Sleep* winning the British Fantasy Award for Best Collection, 2017.

Imaginarium adapted *The Ritual* and *No One Gets Out Alive* into feature films and more of his work is currently in development for the screen.

The author lives in Devon, England. More information about the author and his books is available at: www.adamlgnevill.com

More Horror Fiction from Adam L. G. Nevill and Ritual Limited.

Available in eBook (and included in Kindle Unlimited) at Amazon, and in paperback and audio from all major online retailers. Signed editions are available from www.adamlgnevill.com

Cunning Folk

No home is heaven with hell next door.

Money's tight and their new home is a fixer-upper. Deep in rural South West England, with an ancient wood at the foot of the garden, Tom and his family are miles from anywhere and anyone familiar. His wife, Fiona, was never convinced that buying the money-pit at auction was a good idea. Not least because the previous owner committed suicide. Though no one can explain why.

Within days of crossing the threshold, when hostilities break out with the elderly couple next door, Tom's dreams of future contentment are threatened by an escalating tit-for-tat campaign of petty damage and disruption.

Increasingly isolated and tormented, Tom risks losing his home, everyone dear to him and his mind. Because, surely, only the mad would suspect that the oddballs across the hedgerow command unearthly powers. A malicious magic even older than the eerie wood and the strange barrow therein. A hallowed realm from where, he suspects, his neighbours draw a hideous power.

A compelling folk-horror story of deadly rivalry and the oldest magic from the four times winner of The August Derleth Award for Best Horror Novel.

"*Cunning Folk* gets under the skin from the first page, the story infused with mordant humour and grotesquely apt images of confinement, frustration and otherworldly power." *Toronto Star.*

"In all, this is a great fast-paced horror read that is perfect for longtime fans of Adam Nevill but also a great introduction to the type of book he usually writes. This gets a solid five out of five from me." *Horror Bound.*

The Reddening

Winner of the August Derleth Award for Best Horror Novel, 2020.

One million years of evolution didn't change our nature. Nor did it bury the horrors predating civilisation. Ancient rites, old deities and savage ways can reappear in the places you least expect.

Lifestyle journalist Katrine escaped past traumas by moving to a coast renowned for seaside holidays and natural beauty. But when a vast hoard of human remains and prehistoric artefacts is discovered in nearby Brickburgh, a hideous shadow engulfs her life.

Helene, a disillusioned lone parent, lost her brother, Lincoln, six years ago. Disturbing subterranean noises he recorded prior to vanishing, draw her to Brickburgh's caves. A site where early humans butchered each other across sixty thousand years. Upon the walls, images of their nameless gods remain.

Amidst rumours of drug plantations and new sightings of the mythical red folk, it also appears that the inquisitive have been disappearing from this remote part of the world for years. A rural idyll where outsiders are unwelcome and where an infernal power is believed to linger beneath the earth. A timeless supernormal influence that only the desperate would dream of confronting. But to save themselves and those they love, and to thwart a crimson tide of pitiless barbarity, Kat and Helene are given no choice. They were involved and condemned before they knew it.

The Reddening is an epic story of folk and prehistoric horrors, written by the author of *The Ritual*, *Last Days*, *No One Gets Out Alive* and the four times winner of The August Derleth Award for Best Horror Novel.

Some Will Not Sleep
Selected Horrors

Winner of the British Fantasy Award: Best Collection 2017.

In ghastly harmony with the nightmarish visions of the award-winning writer's novels, these stories blend a lifelong appreciation of horror culture with the grotesque fascinations and terrors that are the author's own. Adam L. G. Nevill's best early horror stories are collected here for the first time.

"Great storytelling, but across a wider palate and range of styles than you might have expected, leading to some delightfully unexpected visions and hellscapes." *Gingernuts of Horror.*

"There is not one single tale which feels less than the others, none which seem to be mere 'filler'. They are beautifully crafted, original and complete works." *This is Horror.*

"In Some Will Not Sleep nothing is sacred, nothing is safe, and goodness me, if you like horror fiction you're going to absolutely love every damn minute." *Pop Mythology.*

Hasty for the Dark
Selected Horrors

Hasty for the Dark is the second short story collection from the award-winning and widely appreciated British writer of horror fiction, Adam L. G. Nevill. The author's best horror stories from 2009 to 2015 are collected here for the first time.

"These tales are dark, starkly violent, but also subtle and ambiguous, often at the same time." *This is Horror.*

"The nine tales are cleverly varied, exhibiting varied pace, chills which deal with the supernatural in both every day and altogether freakier situations, and other curve-balls which drop feet into other genres." *Gingernuts of Horror.*

"His stories weave their way inside of your head and plant seeds of doubt and terror. He is a master of creating oppressive, creepy atmospheres and of taking your imagination to places you would rather he didn't." *The Grim Reader.*

Wyrd and Other Derelictions

Derelictions are horror stories told in ways you may not have encountered before. Something is missing from the silent places and worlds inside these stories. Something has been removed, taken flight, or been destroyed. Us.

Derelictions are weird tales that tell of aftermaths and of new and liminal places. Each location has witnessed catastrophe, infernal visitations, or unearthly transformations. But across these landscapes of murder, genocide and invasion, crucial evidence remains. And it is the task of the reader to sift through ruin and ponder the residual enigma, to behold and wonder at the full horror that was visited upon mankind.
Wyrd' contains seven derelictions, original tales of mystery and horror from the author of *Hasty for the Dark* and *Some Will Not Sleep* (winner of The British Fantasy Award for Best Collection).

"This is a different collection, one that might remind one of Peter Straub, Thomas Ligotti, or even Robert Aickman in its exquisite weirdness. It is well worth the read. Recommended reading for any serious horror fan or for speculative fiction aficionados who crave intelligence in their weirdness." *Cemetery Dance.*

"I can't recommend this collection of stories enough. This is experimental literary horror and the experiment has exceeded all expectations. Read this and enjoy the horrific scenes Nevill has laid out for you." *Horror Bound.*

"Nevill guides us through ruined landscapes and describes the aftermath . . . then leaves it to the reader to piece together what happened. Each of these derelictions left me unsettled and I couldn't put the collection down. 5 Stars." *Deadhead Reviews.*

Free eBook

If you like horror stories, missing chapters, advice for writing horror, articles on horror fiction and films, and much more, register at www.adamlgnevill.com to seize your Free Book today.